THE NIGHT RAVEN

CROW INVESTIGATIONS: BOOK ONE

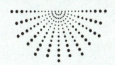

SARAH PAINTER

Siskin
Press

This is a work of fiction. Names, characters, organisations, places, events, and incidents are either products of the author's imagination or are used fictitiously. Any resemblance to actual persons, living or dead, or actual events, is purely coincidental.

Published by Siskin Press Limited

Cover Design by Stuart Bache

ALSO BY SARAH PAINTER

The Language of Spells

The Secrets of Ghosts

The Garden of Magic

In The Light of What We See

Beneath The Water

The Lost Girls

The Crow Investigations Series

The Silver Mark

The Fox's Curse

The Pearl King

The Copper Heart

The Shadow Wing

The Broken Cage

For Team Painter,
with all my love.

Come, the croaking raven doth
bellow for revenge.

— HAMLET, WILLIAM SHAKESPEARE

CHAPTER ONE

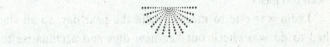

Lydia Crow stood on a wet pavement in London and peered through the grimy front window of The Fork cafe. Her view was obscured by dingy nets and a couple of posters which had been cheekily stuck on the glass, but she cupped hands around her eyes and put her face dangerously close to the smeared surface. It was dark inside, of course, but she could make out the shapes of tables and chairs and a counter at the back.

When Uncle Charlie had mailed her a set of keys and told her it was time she joined the Family business, Lydia had told him very firmly that she was going to do no such thing. Three months later, though, after a surveillance job that had turned out to be unpleasantly complicated, she rethought the gesture. Her boss, Karen, had just told her to take a few weeks away from Aberdeen, for the good of her own health and well-being, when Uncle Charlie had shown his usual uncanny sense of timing and called her to offer a place to stay in London. When he rang, using the mobile number she didn't know he had, Charlie made it sound as if she would be doing him a favour. He said that he needed her help. That, more to the point, the Family needed her help.

He wouldn't give details over the phone and was almost certainly lying, but at that point Lydia no longer cared. She needed a change of scenery and didn't have the funds to go anywhere else. Now, inhaling the familiar scent of exhaust fumes and drains, mixed with the faint tang of blood from the Camberwell market, she wondered whether she had been too hasty.

Lydia was due to meet Charlie the next day, so all she had to do was check out her new digs and acclimatise to being back in London. Not that one night was enough time for the latter. Lydia stepped away from the window and looked for another door. There wasn't one. Some scallywag had added a spray-painted 'ed' to the end of the word 'Fork' on the faded signage, but the number of the building was the same as the tag on the set of keys. This was the right place.

'Somewhere to stay. A little favour.' Uncle Charlie hadn't lied. He just hadn't given her the full details. It was Lydia's fault for assuming it would be a domestic residence, not a disused cafe. The building had four floors, though; maybe there was a flashy little flat with a roof garden just waiting for her up the stairs? Maybe.

Lydia pulled out her phone, still looking up at the building. 'I don't know anything about running a cafe,' Lydia said when Charlie answered.

'Lydia, sweetheart.' Uncle Charlie's voice was warm and, despite herself, Lydia felt a glow.

'If this is what you need help with, I'm not your girl,' Lydia ploughed on. 'You said a quick favour, this is not a permanent move, just a quick visit –'

'You need a place to stay, right?'

'Right, but…'

'So stay at the cafe. It's been closed for months and there's a flat upstairs. Open it up, don't open it up. Makes no difference to me.'

Lydia opened her mouth to ask about rent but Charlie was still talking, his voice had the persuasive note that made him so successful in business. The tone that made some people in the Family say he could almost have been born a Silver. Although they said it very quietly, of course.

'You'll be doing me a favour. A legit tenant. Little start-up. Looks good on the books.'

'I thought I was already doing you a favour. This mysterious problem you need help –'

Charlie spoke across her. 'Not on the phone.' And he cut the connection.

And there was the sinking feeling. Favours in her family never came for free. Lydia knew there would be something to pay down the line and, despite everyone in the Family knowing she was officially 'out', that something might well be illegal, but what choice did she have? At this point in time it was Uncle Charlie's undoubtedly poisoned chalice or moving back home with her parents. The latter was the sensible option, of course. Except that it had been hard enough to leave the first time, and Lydia wasn't sure she could do it again. Plus, she worried that a few weeks of home comforts would be some powerful motivation-sapping mojo and, instead of heading back to Aberdeen and her job, she would start joining her mother for bridge and never, ever leave. Not to mention the fact that it was bad enough that she was back from Scotland and kind of in hiding, she didn't want to compound the embarrassment by crawling back to her childhood bedroom. She could bunk at the cafe for a few weeks, sort out Charlie's imaginary problem, and wait out her own professional snafu until it was safe to head back to Scotland.

The black paint on the front door was peeling, but the lock was top of the line and shiny bright. Charlie must have just had it replaced and Lydia was touched. He was looking after her security, and that was a nice feeling.

The warm and fuzzies didn't last long, however. The place was a dump. She snapped on the lights and the harsh strip bulbs revealed nicotine-yellow walls, plastic-topped tables and a floor that looked as if it was developing sentient life.

There was a counter along the back wall with a door which presumably opened onto the kitchen. Lydia knew she ought to check it out, see if she would at least have working appliances to feed herself while she worked out her next move, but she didn't feel strong enough. Judging by the state of the front, the kitchen would be filthy. And a filthy kitchen would've attracted vermin. You were never far from a rat in London, Lydia knew, but she had absolutely no desire to have this confirmed with visual evidence.

A door to the left of the counter was marked with male and female symbols and a laminated sign was blue-tacked underneath. 'Toilets are for the use of patrons only.'

Lydia had been hoping for a side-entrance to the flat above, a private access of some kind that would mean she didn't have to come through the deserted cafe, but the price was right and it was only for a week or so. She could live with this creepy entrance for that long. Still, the dead air of the empty cafe seemed to bunch behind her as she opened the door, like a creature coiled and ready to pounce.

There was a narrow flight of stairs covered in industrial linoleum. Framed black and white pictures of Camberwell's past lined the walls and there were three doors leading off a small landing. Two were clearly the toilets and the third was marked 'private'. The stairs continued up, the lino giving way to brown carpet. Lydia opened the door, clocking a bare office space. There was a desk with a boxy computer monitor that looked like a reject from the nineties with trailing wires and no keyboard. A broken metal Venetian blind at the window, its slats all bent and covered in thick dust, completed an

4

interior design aesthetic that screamed 'economic downturn'.

Lydia closed the door on the depressing tableau and continued up the stairs, trying not to care too much about the horrible brown carpet and musty, unused air which was wafting over her face. Karen's offices were bright and clean and smelled of neroli oil, and Lydia's flat in Aberdeen had an entire wall of bookshelves and oak flooring. She had sat in her living room and stared at those shelves, feeling like she had finally made it as a proper, successful adult. 'Suck it up, buttercup,' Lydia said out loud, trying to raise her spirits. Her voice sounded odd in the dead air making her feel even worse.

The stairs opened onto a landing with a single door. It had to be the entrance to the flat but there was nothing to indicate that this was the entrance to a separate dwelling, apart from an electric doorbell fixed to the wall. Lydia pressed it experimentally and heard it buzz inside. She tried the handle and the door swung open. *No lock. Super.* Lydia made a mental note to speak to Charlie about security.

Inside the flat was a short hallway and an archway leading to more stairs. One door revealed a small bathroom with a shower cubicle and white fittings, while the open door at the end led to a large living room. It had a tall sash window and an old fireplace which needed a good scrub. There was a low sofa and an IKEA folding chair leaned against one wall and that was it. Cosy. Lydia focused on the window as it was truly the best thing about the room and tried not to think too hard about the stains on the hard green carpet. After staring out at the street for as long as possible, reminding herself that there was a world outside of this musty-smelling hell hole, she felt strong enough to continue exploring.

Off the living room there was a doorway to a small galley kitchen. Braced for filth, Lydia was pleased to find it was basically bare and dusty with plain white units, stainless steel round sink and a speckled-grey, laminate worktop.

The final door led to a bedroom that was more of a cupboard with a bare single bed and small chest of drawers. Suddenly, the tiredness from her ten-hour drive hit, and she felt her resolve weaken. She felt the weight of the dead air and wanted to hear a human voice.

Her mother answered immediately. 'Lydia? Are you all right?'

'I'm great,' Lydia said, taking the stairs on up. 'I'm back down south, just wanted to let you know.'

'Are you coming home?' Lydia could hear the mix of hope and worry in her mum's voice. It reminded her why she was staying in this charmless flat instead of heading home.

'Kind of,' Lydia said. 'I'm staying in town.'

'For how long?'

'Don't know, yet. Look, mum, I don't want you to hear this from anyone else so –'

'You're pregnant?'

'No! Mum!'

'Sorry, sorry. But you know, it wouldn't be so shocking.'

'I'm staying above an old cafe. It's a disused building.' She had reached the landing and there were no more stairs. She was on the top floor of the building and the ceilings were lower, here, in what had probably originally been attic space or servants' quarters.

'You're squatting?' Her mum's voice was bemused rather than out-right disapproving and Lydia felt a rush of love for her. She heard another voice in the background and her mother broke away from the conversation to say 'it's Lydia,'.

'It's nothing illegal,' Lydia said. 'Uncle Charlie –'

'Tell me you're not with Charles.' Her mother's voice, usually so gentle and warm, was suddenly harsh with fear.

'I'm not with Uncle Charlie,' Lydia said, pushing open a

door. The main bedroom was directly above the living room. It had a smaller version of the window in the room below and a double bed with new sheets, pillows and a duvet all still in their plastic packaging sitting on top of the mattress. She wasn't lying. She wasn't with Uncle Charlie at that exact moment.

'Oh, thank God.' She heard her mother turn away from the phone and repeat the words for her father's benefit. 'She's not with him!'

'Sorry, darling,' her mother said. 'You'd never do anything like that, I know.'

'I need a place to stay and he's letting me kip here until I work out my next move.'

'Well that's ridiculous,' her mum said. 'You can stay here. You don't need to be in Camberwell. It's not safe.'

'It's more convenient to be in town,' Lydia said, feeling like hell.

'Convenient for what? You just said you don't know what you're doing.'

'It's fine,' Lydia said, knowing what would be worrying her mum. 'No strings. I don't have to do anything in return. I'm doing him a favour by living here, keeping an eye on the place.'

'The day your uncle does anything from the good of his heart will be a cold day in hell with pigs flying past the window and the dead getting up from their graves.'

'I know,' Lydia said, irritation breaking through. 'I'm not an idiot.'

'And we know that, darling. But you mustn't try to play his game. He'll make you think you're carrying all the cards and then he'll rob you blind.'

'Uncle Charlie loves me,' Lydia said, almost sure that was true.

'Of course he does!' Her mum sounded properly offended. 'Everyone in the family loves you.'

'Well, then,' Lydia began, but her mum interrupted. 'But that won't stop him.'

Lydia had been brought up away from her extended family. Her parents had been all-too-aware of how her assorted uncles and cousins would view any kind of ability, even one as muted as Lydia's, and they didn't want any of them taking liberties. When Lydia had asked what they'd meant by that, they'd shaken their heads in tight-lipped unison.

'But they're family. Uncle Charlie is your brother,' Lydia had said, once she'd grown into a bolshie teen.

Her dad had smiled very sadly. 'I love my brother and Charlie is probably the best of them, but he's a Family man first and foremost. Always has been. He'd use you as soon as blinking, just like the others.' Then her usually mild dad had become uncharacteristically intense. 'Don't ever tell him what you can do, okay? He loves you but he'll still find a way to use you and I don't want you mixed up in all that.'

It hadn't been an issue. Lydia, for all her curiosity, hadn't wanted to get mixed up in Crow Family business, either. That way lay scary-looking-men and women, the various aunts and cousins, who appeared either worn-out or far scarier than their heavily-muscled husbands. She wasn't a kid anymore, though, or a rebellious teen. She was a grown woman with a limited skill-set, cash-flow issues and a strong desire to make over her life.

She took a final look around the bedroom, deciding this was where she would sleep. She dropped her rucksack onto the bed and opened the window to let in some fresh air. It definitely had potential and, thankfully, stripped floorboards rather than manky carpet. Feeling cheered, Lydia pushed open the door across the landing and stopped. The third bedroom had a sharp, citrusy scent which was oddly familiar. There was another double bed, made up with navy-striped linen and a couple of framed film posters on the wall. On the far wall, there was a glass door with a voile curtain half-pulled across it. Lydia took a couple of steps into the room, feeling as if she was trespassing on someone's private abode. Which was stupid. The flat was empty. The cafe had been deserted for six months at least. Unless there was a squatter. Lydia reached into her pocket for her mobile. She didn't want to run to Charlie for every little thing, but maybe he'd let another stray relative stay here and then forgotten to tell her. She ought to check before calling the police. Before she could look at the screen, she felt the hairs rise on the back of her neck. There was someone behind her, she could feel their gaze. She forced herself to turn around, mouth already opening to scream but the room was empty. There was nobody there. The door was half open, revealing an equally person-free landing.

She was jumpy. Being back in London and alone in this deserted old wreck was playing havoc with her imagination. That was all. She turned back and shouted in surprise. There was a man standing by the wardrobe on the far side of the bed. He was wearing a boxy pale grey jacket with the sleeves rolled up. He had lightly tanned forearms, blue eyes and a lot of golden blonde hair which was shining in the light from the window.

'Bloody hell, you scared me,' Lydia said, her fear flipping to anger in an instant. He must have been hiding behind the bed when she walked in. 'What are you playing at?'

The man looked as shocked as she felt, his mouth hung open and there was a confused, frozen-look on his face. Then he said: 'I live here. Who are you?'

There was something odd about his voice but Lydia didn't have time to think about it. The smell of citrus was stronger, too, and she knew that was something important.

'Lydia Crow. My uncle owns this place. He didn't tell me about you.'

'I see,' the man said. He was around her age, Lydia

thought. Maybe even younger. She had thought he was older first because of the weird jacket. It was paired with matching grey trousers and shiny shoes. Most blokes Lydia knew wore T-shirts, jeans and trainers.

She crossed her arms and gave him her hard stare. She expected him to introduce himself and to spin some line about being the friend of a friend, or Charlie letting him stay here or something, but he didn't say a word. He just stared back at her in wide-eyed terror as if she were the one lurking in supposed-to-be empty buildings and scaring people half to death.

Citrus. Her brain was trying to tell her something. That scent which had the sharp tang of lemon but also something like smoke. Not cigarette or wood smoke, but definitely something burned. She hadn't smelled it for years. Not since she had seen Grandma Crow attending her own funeral.

Lydia opened her mouth to ask 'are you real?' when a noise from behind made her turn around. There was another man standing in the open doorway of the bedroom. This one was wearing a black T-shirt, tight over bulging muscles. He had close-cropped hair and a nose that looked like it had been broken more than once. He was also holding a gun and was pointing it straight at Lydia.

CHAPTER TWO

Lydia had never even seen a gun in real life, much less had one aimed at her, and she felt an unpleasant liquid sensation in her stomach. The feeling headed further south and the thought of wetting herself – actually, truly wetting herself – was enough to make her tense her muscles and avert disaster. A small part of her brain was insisting that she ought to worry more about the gunman than an embarrassing wet patch, but she ignored it so that she didn't pass out from terror.

'Sit down please.' The man indicated the bed by lifting his chin. 'Time for a talk.'

Bedroom. Gunman. Bed. This did not sound like a good idea. This sounded like the horrible details in some tragic and violent news story. The thug didn't look hurried. He didn't look excited or nervous, either. He didn't look bored, exactly, but this was clearly not his first day at Bad Guy school. Lydia had been protected from the worst of her extended family, but she'd still met a few professionals at weddings, christenings and so on. They had the same dead-eye look.

'Come on, now,' the man said, gently enough, and Lydia

realised something: He was going to kill her. She wondered if Grey Jacket knew the gun man. Why hadn't he said anything? She glanced across, hoping to find solidarity, maybe even comfort, but instead she found the wardrobe. Jacket-boy had gone. Had he dived underneath the bed in fear? She didn't blame him, but hoped to God he was dialling 999 from down there.

Lydia tried to make her legs move. She wanted to obey the man, not to give him any reason to hurt her, but her feet felt stuck to the carpet.

The gunman was looking around and his gaze caught on something behind Lydia. 'Open the door,' he said.

For a moment, Lydia didn't know what he was taking about. He was standing in the doorway. Then she remembered the glass door and turned around. The path to the door would lead them both to the other side of the bed. If jacket-boy was hiding there, he wasn't going to stay safe for long. Lydia moved toward the door, anyway, not seeing any other option. When she got around the end of the bed she forced herself not to glance down, not wanting to give away jacket-boy's position on the slim hope that the gunman was going to stay on the other side of the room.

'Open it slowly,' the man said. His voice was deep and expressionless and his accent oddly neutral. Lydia knew that she ought to be filing away details, her training with Karen had included advanced observation, but her brain seemed to be randomly firing. An image of her mother's face, frowning as she piped wobbly writing onto Lydia's tenth birthday cake, was followed by the thought that the voile curtain was a horrible peach colour, and that the door would almost certainly be locked. It wasn't. The double-glazed door swung smoothly outward and the sudden rush of cool fresh air cleared Lydia's mind a little. He was going to make her go outside, onto what Lydia could now see was a small roof terrace with a black iron railing running along its edge.

The man was right behind her, she could smell his deodorant. He pressed the muzzle of the gun into the small of her back. 'We're going outside. Don't make a sound.'

Lydia stepped over the door frame and down a single step onto the paved surface of the terrace. She was aware of the grey sky stretching above, the roof scape to her left and right with a forest of chimney pots, and the red brick facade of the building. The house next door had a taller roof with a steeper pitch and a couple of dormer windows jutting out. They had built over their terrace space and there wasn't a window facing onto where Lydia was standing, just the smooth masonry of the extension. She wondered whether anybody was home and if it was worth screaming. Would they hear her? And if they did, would they bother to call the police?

Her legs were shaking and she cursed her weakness. Think, Lydia, don't wobble. *Think.*

'Forward,' the thug said from behind her. 'Six steps.'

In an odd way, Lydia appreciated the man's specificity. It made it feel as if she just followed his detailed instructions, all would be well. A second later, she realised that this was probably a technique. Maybe something you learned in assassin school.

'You don't have to do this. I can give you money.' Lydia hated the thin sound of her voice. The pleading. Crows didn't plead.

He pressed a little with the gun and Lydia walked toward the railing. There was a yard below, the tops of wheelie bins visible and a wall with an access gate. A narrow road ran behind the terrace and, facing Lydia, were the backs of another row of buildings. These ones didn't have balconies or roof gardens and the windows that she could see had obscured glass or closed blinds. Nobody to see. Nobody to call the police. Or Charlie.

'My family' Lydia began, the fear full and cold, now,

13

filling every part of her mind. He wasn't here to steal from the house. He wasn't here for money or information. He was here to kill her.

The gun was no longer pressing against her back, but that was scant comfort when she knew it was there. A mechanical assemblage of steel that could stop the heart that was currently beating wildly in her chest.

'Climb over the railing,' he said.

'What?' Lydia's mind was stuttering, still not making sense.

'You're going to jump. Suicide.'

'I don't think so,' Lydia said. She turned around. He was a couple of paces away, now, the gun still steadily trained upon her.

'But, yes,' he said. 'Up and over. Let's see if you can fly.'

Lydia thought of her parents, then. And Charlie and every family story she had ever been told. She might be a weak member of the Family, might have been brought up outside the nest and be something of a genetic freak, but she wasn't going to dishonour the Family name. Crows did not die easily. They fought, beak and claw.

'No.'

He shrugged. 'Turn around.'

'No,' Lydia said, the word coming more easily this time. She wanted to see her killer. To look him in the eye and make him do the same as he took her life.

At that moment, the man in the grey jacket appeared behind the gunman. He just appeared. Materialised. Before Lydia could feel surprised about that, he had hit the man with the gun over the back of the head with a large terra-cotta pot held in both hands.

The gunman folded forwards, his legs crumpling so that his knees and face both hit the paving stone at the same time. It made a crunching sound and there was a spray of blood.

14

Jacket-boy dropped his weapon and it broke in two, spilling dry earth. Lydia was looking at the blood and the gun, which was still in the man's hand. She knew this was her moment. She should jump on his back, try to grab the gun, but the idea of getting closer to the enormous man, to attempting to touch that evil piece of metal, seemed utterly impossible.

Also impossible was the speed with which he was recovering. Already he was on his hands and knees, blood pouring from his face, his teeth bared in a grimace as he staggered upright. He began to raise the gun, again, and Lydia dived to the side, hoping to get to the door, to run far and fast.

Jacket-boy shoved him and he staggered forward, taking steps to keep his balance. Jacket-boy shoved again, a look of fear, concentration and weird joy on his face. It sent a cold spike down Lydia's spine. In a split second, the gun man was hitting the railing, his momentum causing his body to fold over it. Lydia ran forward. Whether to push him over or stop him from falling, she had no conscious idea. She only knew that it was a moment of opportunity.

Before she reached him, Jacket-boy was there. He was lifting and shoving and, quicker than Lydia could believe possible, the big man's centre of gravity altered and he went over the railing. One second he was there, his stomach on top of the railing and then his thighs, his feet lifting, and then he wasn't there at all. He let out a sound as he fell. Halfway between a shout and a scream and then there was a sickening thud, followed by another.

Lydia looked at jacket-boy in shock.

'I did it,' he said, his voice echoing strangely as if he was in a tiny room, not the open air. Then he disappeared.

Lydia looked over the railing, very carefully and without touching the metal. The man was spread-eagled on the street below, his legs at terrible angles and a pool of blood

15

spreading from beneath. The green wheelie bin was over on its side, plastic bottles, lids, and rusty tins spilled onto the ground.

She pulled her phone from her back pocket and called 999. Police. Ambulance. All the emergency services. Please come quickly.

Her mind was starting to work again, although her thoughts were still fragmented. Coldness flowed over her body and her stomach clenched. She leaned over as the bile rose. It was mostly liquid and Lydia remembered that she hadn't eaten yet that day. She had been too tense; coming back home had felt oddly dangerous. Turned out her instincts were bang on.

At once, she couldn't stay on the terrace a second longer. Lydia went through the door, back into the bedroom. She sat on the bed and wrapped her arms around her body, hugging tightly. How long before the police and ambulance arrived? Was he dead? She was suddenly seized with renewed terror. That he wasn't lying on the ground, bleeding and immobile, that he had somehow got up and was moving back through the house, coming to kill her. Like The Terminator.

A jolt of adrenaline spiked through Lydia and she was up and moving. Back on the terrace and to the railing. The man was still lying in the same position. Out cold. Or dead. Lydia sunk down to the paving stone and held onto the black iron of the railing. A pigeon landed on the terrace and she watched it strut around, concentrating on the grey bird and its stupid jutting neck action so that she didn't have to think about anything else.

The sound of sirens. Lydia forced herself upright again. The pigeon flapped away and Lydia's eye was caught by something else. The broken terracotta pot lying in two pieces with the mess of soil spilling across the floor. There had been a man in a grey jacket and he had hit the man with the gun. The man with the jacket had appeared and disappeared right in front of her. He had saved her life.

Lydia went downstairs to meet the police who were now parked in the street below. There were flashing lights of an ambulance and the sounds of heavy shoes on tarmac, people talking, radios, sirens.

Lydia held onto the bannister as she walked down the stairs. She was being careful as she didn't want to fall. She also was being careful in her thoughts. She wasn't thinking about the gun man who was lying in the street, surrounded by his own blood. She wasn't thinking about how close she had come to death in the last half an hour. Instead, she thought about the man who had saved her life. She knew, of course, why jacket-boy's voice sounded weird. She knew why it was a familiar weirdness. He was a ghost.

LATER, sitting in the back of the second ambulance with a blanket around her shoulders and a paramedic taking her pulse, Lydia tried to organise what she was going to say about jacket-boy. She could hardly explain that a poltergeist had saved her life.

'She's good,' the paramedic said to an approaching officer who turned and nodded to somebody else, somebody out of Lydia's sight-line.

The man who stepped up, then, wasn't in uniform. Obviously a higher-up type. He was also very tall.

'How are you feeling?'

'Is he dead?'

The broken-looking thug had been loaded onto the first ambulance and it had left with the siren and lights going. Lydia thought that meant he was still alive, but she wasn't sure.

The man shook his head. 'I'm DCI Fleet. I'm the senior investigating officer. And you are-'

'Lydia,' Lydia had already given her name to a female officer. Moorhouse. She had patted her on the arm and told her they would speak to her once the paramedics had finished checking her over.

'Lydia Crow,' DCI Fleet said. 'Is that correct?'

'Yes,' Lydia said.

'Can you tell me what happened?'

'He had a gun,' Lydia said. 'He walked me out onto the terrace and tried to get me over the railing. I struggled and he went over instead.'

Fleet's expression remained neutral. 'Did the gun fire?'

'No,' Lydia said.

'Can you show me where this happened?'

LYDIA HATED BEING on the terrace. The thought that she had gained a roof terrace but that she would never want to use it ran through her mind as she pointed out the railings to Fleet and Constable Moorhouse.

'Was that involved in the altercation?' Moorhouse pointed to the broken terracotta pot.

Lydia hesitated. The medics would surely notice he had been hit over the back of the head with something heavy. But her fingerprints wouldn't be on the pot. Would they take fingerprints? Wasn't she the victim in this situation? She shook her head. 'He made me walk over here,' she pointed.

The tall cop didn't seem overly interested in the railings, he was looking around the terrace. After a thorough search of the space, his gaze found Lydia again and rested there. He had brown eyes and, while they were perfectly attractive from a purely aesthetic viewpoint, they were calculating and Lydia shifted her feet and looked away. And then wondered if that made her look guilty.

'Do you need to sit down?'

It wasn't what she was expecting him to say and she felt her knees buckle as if they had been given permission.

The female officer stepped forward. 'Ms Crow, why don't we step downstairs. Have a cup of tea and we can chat there.'

Within minutes, Lydia found herself sat on the slightly sticky leatherette banquette of one of the booths in the window of the cafe. There was a large paper cup in front of her with steam escaping through the hole in the plastic lid. Someone, maybe the police constable, had gone to the nearest proper cafe and bought her a tea. Lydia blinked back sudden tears at this simple piece of kindness.

'I just need to take a statement,' constable Moorhouse said, apologetically. 'Then we'll leave you in peace. A sleep can be good after something like this.'

Lydia wondered if she spoke from personal experience. 'That's fine,' Lydia wrapped her hands around the tea, feeling comforted by its warmth.

The constable got Lydia to go over the events, asking questions until the small sequence was clear. 'Did you hear the man come into the building?'

'No,' Lydia shook her head. 'I was just looking around the place, getting my bearings. I was in the bedroom and –' Lydia stopped speaking. She had been in the bedroom and she had seen a ghost. 'I turned around and he was there. In the doorway. With a gun.'

Moorhouse made a note. 'Did he say what he wanted?'

Lydia swallowed, shook her head.

'Did you recognise him?'

Another head shake. Lydia drank some tea and gave it a little more thought. He had reminded her of some of the Family's associates but just because of his air of power and intensity. She didn't think she had ever seen him before.

The door to the flat swung open and Fleet appeared,

19

filling the room with his presence. He grabbed a cup from the cardboard tray and nodded at Moorhouse.

She stood up immediately. 'That will do for today. We will need to take a formal statement but I can see you are very shaken up and it can wait.'

Lydia stood up, too. She held a hand out, relieved that the conversation was over but also not entirely ready to be alone.

'I'll be out in a second,' Fleet said to Moorhouse's retreating back.

She looked at her watch and was surprised at how little time had passed. An hour at most since she had unlocked the door to her new home. 'A new record,' she said.

'Sorry?'

'For things to turn bad,' Lydia said. 'It's a speciality of mine.'

He smiled, the crinkles around his eyes spreading out and making him look entirely different. 'I don't think this one counts,' he said. 'It's not your fault.'

Lydia focused on him properly, noticing for the first time that, in addition to being tall and hiding a good set of shoulders inside his suit jacket, there was a kind of glow about him. A gleam.

'Have you lived here long?' He pulled out a small notebook and Lydia's heart sank. More questions.

'I just arrived today,' Lydia said. 'Is that part of the statement?'

He shook his head, smiling a little. 'Just interested, sorry. Used to come here all the time with my aunt. When I was little.'

Lydia couldn't picture the man in front of her as anything approaching 'little'.

'It used to smell so good.' He shook his head, as if clearing it.

'Well,' Lydia said, suddenly feeling defensive. 'I only moved in today. It's derelict.'

'You've taken on a project, all right,' he nodded at the upturned chairs.

'It's not my project,' Lydia said. 'I'm just staying for a week or two. Then I'll go home.'

'Scotland, right?' He managed to make it sound like 'Narnia'. Like she was delusional to believe that such a place existed.

Lydia waited to see if he was going to say something else, but he just tapped his pencil onto the surface of his notebook, before flipping it shut. 'Okay, then. If you think of anything else...'

'I'll let you know.' Lydia said.

'You do that.'

He put the notebook away. 'Thank you for your cooperation, Miss Crow.'

'Thank you for coming,' Lydia said and then wanted to smack herself. This wasn't a bloody tea party.

'Give my regards to your uncle,' Fleet said, pausing at the door.

'My uncle?'

'Charlie Crow. He owns this place, doesn't he?'

'How do you know that?'

'I'm a local,' he said, fixing her with a hard look. 'Born and bred.'

Lydia got the warning loud and clear. He knew her family. Her spirits sank even lower.

ALONE AGAIN, Lydia locked the front door, using the bolt at the top as well as the key. Then she went upstairs to the bedroom. She knew that if she didn't do it straight away she would chicken out and have to get the train to the suburbs

21

and move into her old bedroom. And she wasn't going to take trouble anywhere near her parents. Her dad was the youngest brother in the Family and, unlike Michael Corleone, he had been allowed to escape the business. He had married a nice girl from Maidstone and built a quiet life out in the suburbs.

The bedroom was empty. Lydia stood in the doorway, feeling stupid, and then said 'hello?' which accomplished nothing except an increase in her personal embarrassment. 'Thank you for hitting him,' she said, anyway. 'And the rest. You saved my life.'

The ghost didn't appear and Lydia didn't hear any voices. The air felt neutral and the citrus smell was just a memory. Just in case, Lydia added. 'I'm going to take the other room. Don't randomly appear in there unless you want me to have a heart attack.'

She closed the door and went up the stairs to her new room, calling Charlie as she did so. 'Somebody just broke in and threatened me.'

Charlie didn't miss a beat. 'You need a cleaning service?'

'No,' Lydia said, wishing she didn't know what that meant. When her Dad had sunk one too many beers on a Saturday afternoon, he'd often opened up with tales from the Crow family archive. They weren't pretty.

'You're all right, though? Not hurt?'

Lydia blinked back sudden tears. 'No. I'm fine.'

Charlie let out a breath. 'Okay, good. Who was it?'

'I don't know,' Lydia said. 'Who knows I'm here?'

'You recognise the guy?'

'I don't know anyone. I only just got here, you know that.' Lydia looked out of the bedroom window while she spoke. The street outside was quiet, pools of yellow light spilling onto the pavement and the shops opposite shuttered and dark.

'Not one of your old clients?'

Lydia pulled the curtains shut. London felt so far away

from her old life that she hadn't even considered that possibility.

'Lyds?'

'I don't think so. He didn't look familiar.' She closed her eyes, conjuring up the gun man. Not young with hair that was either shaved off or non-existent to start with. Anywhere between forty and sixty, with tanned skin and small eyes.

'Family?'

Lydia knew he didn't mean their family, he meant one of the three others which operated in London. Suggesting that one of the other three London Families had attacked a Crow could spark a war, and Lydia was shaking her head before saying 'no, no, I don't think so.' Lydia was lying. She knew beyond a shadow of a doubt that the gun man hadn't been Pearl, Crow, Silver or Fox. Sensing things like that was the grand extent of her Crow Family magic, but she had promised her dad a long time ago that she would never, ever reveal it to Charlie. Or to anyone in the Family, for that matter. Lydia didn't know if it was embarrassment on her Dad's part or his tendency to be over-protective.

'I'll find out,' Charlie said, sounding grim. Lydia knew that nobody in their right mind would threaten a member of their family unless they were riding in a tank. She didn't want to admit it, but it was comforting to hear Charlie's voice and know that the word would be out, that the protection that came from being a Crow was still in force. When she had been in Aberdeen she had been alone, maybe not entirely off the radar, but definitely on the periphery. Coming back to the city meant diving back into a world she had always been taught to be scared of. Now Lydia wondered whether her over-protective parents had, perhaps, had a point.

. . .

23

Lydia unwrapped the linen from its plastic packaging and began making the bed, thinking hard. If the man wasn't Family then he must be very good at his job. You didn't work as a pro and reach middle-age unless you were highly skilled or had protection of your own. Lydia felt herself shiver again, her hands shaking as she pulled and tucked the sheets. She shrugged off her leather jacket and peeled off her skinny jeans and climbed in. Just as she thought that perhaps she would be able to sleep, she remembered the important detail she had neglected to ask Charlie. Lydia leaned out of bed and released her phone from her jeans pocket, then tapped out a message.

Do you know DCI Fleet?

A moment later her phone rang.

Charlie's voice was sharp. 'You called the police?'

'Obviously,' Lydia said, holding the phone to her ear and staring at the ceiling.

'Interesting choice,' Charlie said, his voice dry. 'You really are your father's kid.'

Lydia stayed silent. She knew that she could have called Charlie instead, and the gun man splattered on the street would have disappeared. The cleaning service would have been swift and untraceable and she wouldn't be giving a formal statement to the police tomorrow, but she would have owed Charlie in ways she didn't want to think about. He was her uncle but he was Family first. Plus, you know, the cleaning service was fatal and that was wrong.

As always, the moral imperative had occurred worryingly low down in her list of concerns. It was one of the many reasons she had always abided by her parents' wishes and stayed out of the Family business. She scared herself.

'Don't worry about Fleet,' Charlie was saying.

'I'm not,' Lydia said. 'Have you found anything about my visitor?'

'He's at the hospital, out cold with broken legs, ribs, arm

24

and spine, and a shattered pelvis. He's also cuffed to the bed, so he definitely won't come at you, again,' Charlie said, satisfaction rich in his voice. 'But he's just a hired hand. I'll let you know when I've traced the head.'

'You don't have to,' Lydia said. 'The less I know –'

'Quite right,' Charlie said, his voice suddenly warm. 'You always were sharp.'

Not that sharp, Lydia thought, putting her mobile onto the floor by the bed. I came back to London.

CHAPTER THREE

Lydia hadn't expected to sleep but PC Moorhouse was absolutely right, ten hours of deep unconsciousness turned out to be just what she needed.

Lydia located a bottle of flavoured water from her rucksack and took a swig in lieu of coffee. It was no substitute, naturally, but she didn't feel quite up to getting up straight away so delicious caffeination would have to wait.

Lydia piled pillows and sat cross-legged on the bed, opening her laptop. First she re-read the emails from her last client, Mr Carter. She was hoping she had imagined the threats as worse than they were. Perhaps she had over-reacted in taking time off from the agency and running down south? London had proved itself not exactly safe as houses and images of frying pans and fires were dancing through her mind. Maybe she could just pack up her stuff and go home... After all, Mr Carter was a respectable business analyst, not a thug.

A quick scan of the emails put paid to that comforting notion. Lydia didn't need to re-read the measured advice from Karen, who had suggested, quite firmly, that she take a week or so 'away' and let things 'simmer down'. Karen had been in the business for thirty years and was unshakeable. When Lydia had questioned whether leaving the country was an over-reaction, Karen had said that Mr Carter had visited the office in person and that Karen thought it wise to use physical distance as a short-term safety measure. 'You've hurt his pride,' she had said. Lydia had objected. Nothing about her investigation had been personal. 'Doesn't matter,' Karen had said. 'He is used to obedience from his subordinates and doesn't like to be contradicted. You exposed part of his life, and confronted his own ideas about himself. He doesn't like to be judged so he is lashing out.'

'I'm not judging him,' Lydia had lied.

'Doesn't matter. He feels like he lost a game and to him, that is unacceptable.'

'Sore losers overturn the board,' Lydia argued, 'they don't suggest they are going to use the dark web to commission a hit on an innocent private investigator.'

Karen had pulled a sympathetic face which, somehow, made the whole situation three hundred times scarier. 'The good news is, his sort get bored easily. He'll move onto something else soon enough. It won't take long for somebody else to piss him off, right enough.'

'Great,' Lydia still couldn't believe one prick of a client could stomp over her life like this.

'Go on a cruise. Visit Paris. Lie on a beach.'

'All at once?'

Karen was already picking up the phone, moving onto the next item. She wasn't being rude or heartless, she was just genuinely busy. It was one of the many things Lydia admired about Karen. Her success. Her work ethic. Her security. One day, Lydia wanted to be the boss. If you were the boss, nobody could fire you.

Back in her temporary bedroom in Camberwell, a cool blast of air brushed past Lydia's cheek, lifting her hair and making the back of her neck prickle. She looked up and let out an annoyingly weak 'ah!'. The jacket-boy was sitting next to her on the bed.

Heart thudding, Lydia managed to release two furious words. 'Get. Away.'

The ghost unfolded from his cross-legged position and stood next to the bed instead, looking hurt. 'Nice 'tude.'

Lydia knew that some of her anger was because she was embarrassed by her fear. After a lifetime of sensing the dead, she had thought herself past that. For as long as she could remember, she had felt the leftover emotions in the air, seen spirits out of the corner of her eye and heard their thin voices in quiet rooms and open spaces. So, this spirit was more corporeal and chatty than any she had ever experienced before, but she liked to think she would have taken his sudden appearance in her stride if she hadn't been worrying about random gunmen and irate cuckolds.

He pushed the sleeves of his vile jacket up to his elbows. Light was spilling from the window onto his face, highlighting its slightly translucent quality, and an expression that appeared to be a battle between hurt and longing.

Lydia swallowed. Beneath her own fear was a strange excitement. Seeing a full spirit like this was something. It wasn't true power, but it was a sign that she was a Crow after all. 'Hello, again.'

'You can still see me?'

'Yep,' Lydia replied. She felt a little bit sick. The way the outline of his clothes and head shimmered was making her feel off balance.

'And you can hear me?'

'I think we've established that.'

He was staring at her. 'You have no idea how this feels...'

His voice seemed less odd but perhaps Lydia was just getting used to it. She tried to think of something to say. What could she ask that wasn't insensitive? Have you lived here long? How did you die? Why are you still hanging around? The spirits of her youth had been shades and feelings, whispers of cold air and voices caught on the very edge of hearing, like badly-tuned radios. She was adrift. 'I'm Lydia,' she said and then remembered that she had already told him that.

'I've never done anything like that before,' he said abruptly.

'Sorry?'

'The shoving thing. And hitting that man. Until yesterday I couldn't even touch anything, let alone lift it. And now –' he reached out and plucked the edge of the curtain. 'Look.'

'Well I'm very grateful,' Lydia said.

'Why aren't you freaking out?' The ghost said. 'I'm freaking out. Why are you so calm?'

Lydia shrugged. 'You're not my first.' The man wasn't looking at her and that made it easier to look at him. He really did look almost solid until he moved, it was unnerving. Every part of Lydia was screaming that he wasn't there at all while her eyes insisted otherwise. 'And I'm not afraid of the dead,' she added. The living were more problematic, in her experience.

'This is weird,' the ghost said. 'I wish I could drink. I could really do with a drink.'

'What's your name?' Lydia said, trying to distract him.

He moved quickly, his outline shimmering in a way which made Lydia's stomach lurch.

'Why do you want to know?'

'Just being friendly,' Lydia said, after swallowing hard.

'I doubt it,' he said. 'No one can be this calm. There is something wrong with you.'

'Hey!'

'How long are you staying?'

'Couple of weeks, probably. At least, that was the plan. Now I'm not sure,' Lydia looked around the room, trying not to picture her attacker bursting through the door. 'Maybe I'll go to Paris.'

The man disappeared and Lydia stopped talking. She stared at the space so recently occupied by something that looked disturbingly like a real person, trying to decide if he had been rude or whether it was a ghost thing. Maybe he couldn't control whether he appeared or not. She felt a shiver of sympathy; it must be awful to be in-between life like that, neither alive nor dead, unable to control or affect anything. Except, of course, that he had. He had saved her life.

Lydia rummaged in her rucksack for her emergency flask and took a swig of whisky to stop her hands from shaking. The alcohol burned her throat as she stayed, staring at the empty space, wondering if the ghost was going to reappear. She thought about taking another nip but knew she didn't really need it and screwed the lid back on. Strange. She felt oddly pleased. Despite being brought up away from the Family, she had always been aware that she was a weak link. There were four magical families left in London and the Crows were the most powerful of them all. At least that's what she had been brought up to believe. They kept their secrets very close to their chests and, since her mum and dad were keen to keep their precious only child as far from that shady world as possible, Lydia was pretty much in the dark as to what those secrets might be.

The Pearls had a facility for selling. They were the original entrepreneurs and their ancestors had run apple carts and bakeries, and had been the first to sell ice cream in the Victorian era and to make money by cutting their flour with dust. Never mind coals to Newcastle, the Pearls could sell shoes to a duck.

The Silver Family had a facility for lying and, unsurprisingly, ran a thriving law firm, and finally there was the Fox Family. Well, the least said about them the better.

Lydia's mobile rang. Emma's number.

'When were you going to phone me, you git?'

'That is spooky, I was just about to,' Lydia said. 'I'm in London.'

'I know, your mum told my mum at bridge last night.'

Emma was Lydia's normal friend from her normal upbringing and she had a normal life. Lydia loved her almost as much for those facts as she did for her sense of humour, kindness and energy.

'It's been madness here,' Emma was saying. 'Archie broke his arm playing football last week and the cat has a hyperthyroid, which is more expensive than it sounds, and the week before that Maise-Maise brought us all the sick bug –'

'Oh no, I'm sorry,' Lydia broke in. She wasn't a good, attentive friend, she knew that. Guilt flooded through her. 'How is Archie doing? Is he okay?'

'He's totally fine. Milking it, now.'

Lydia could hear the smile in her friend's voice and she felt the familiar rush of love, admiration and confusion that her best mate, her old partner in crime, was now a mother. Responsible for tiny human lives. A finder of gym kits, a giver-of-medicine and all that. Emma had been a bit scatty, very sarcastic and a lover of late nights and afternoon naps. When she had turned away from clubbing and travelling and a career to get married and have her first baby aged just twenty-two, Lydia had been incredulous, but Emma was so warm and loving with her kids that Lydia felt as if she was witnessing a whole other, unexpected room in her friend's personality. An entire wing that she hadn't known existed.

Emma stopped the Archie-and-Maisie update and took a breath. 'So, what's new with you?'

'Not much,' Lydia said. 'I'm back in town for a while, though, if you want to meet up.' She held the phone away from her ear while Emma screamed her approval for the suggestion.

Hanging up, Lydia realised she was smiling. There were advantages to running away from Aberdeen and steady employment, after all. And the steady employment had been boring-as-hell until it had become scary-as-hell. Why had nobody warned her that being a private investigator was zero glamour, ninety-nine per cent boredom and one per cent fear-for-your-life? Okay, her boss had told her that on her first day but she hadn't been listening. Lydia knew that she had been drifting through her twenties, failing to work out what she wanted to do with her life, but since that was what your twenties were for, she wasn't too concerned. Apart from the notable exceptions (like married-to-man-of-her-dreams and living-in-domestic-heaven Emma), flailing and falling was on trend and nothing she needed to worry about until she was at least twenty-nine. Or maybe thirty.

But here she was, back in London, and feeling optimistic. Weirdly optimistic. Perhaps the fear last night had masked a small stroke?

LYDIA DEFINITELY NEEDED CAFFEINE, now. The cupboards in the little kitchen were bare so she trailed downstairs to check the cafe. Her hand was on the swing door to the kitchen when she heard a noise. From inside. She pulled her mobile out and dialled the first two nines, her finger ready on the third digit. Perhaps it was ghost-boy. Maybe he was testing out his new-found lifting powers by fixing himself a little snack.

Then she caught what she was about to do – investigate a strange noise the day after she was attacked in the exact same building. Not smart, Lyds. She was just about to retrace her footsteps, get the hell out of the cafe and call the police from a safe location, when she heard a weird sound. Singing. Well, humming really. Just a brief snatch in a voice that was low, female, and had a good tone, even through the door.

Lydia hesitated for a moment more. Her senses weren't telling her to be afraid and she was damned if she was going to spend the rest of her life jumping at shadows. She squared her shoulders and pushed open the door.

There was a person next to the stainless steel counter. A person with a hairnet and an enormous spliff.

The woman was tucking dreads inside the hairnet. She had a navy blue apron with white writing across the bib which read 'Papa Joe's Kitchen'.

Lydia wanted to say 'who the Hell are you?' but there was something intimidating about the woman which made her modify it to 'who are you?'

'Charlie hired me,' she said, her attention firmly on her hair. 'Are you my kitchen assistant?'

'I live here,' Lydia said. 'At the moment. I'm sorry, but there has been a mistake. I don't need a cook. I'm not opening the cafe, just looking after the building for a few weeks.'

The woman shrugged, stubbing out her spliff into a foil container and tucking it into her apron pocket.

Lydia was momentarily flummoxed by the woman's calm silence. She said: 'I'm going to call Charlie, get this sorted out.'

'You gotta do what you gotta do.' The woman turned and bent, lifting a crate onto the metal work surface and commenced unpacking ingredients.

'Don't do that,' Lydia said, as firmly as she could manage. 'This is not a business and I'm not employing anybody. How did you get in here, anyway? The door was locked.'

The woman continued unpacking as if Lydia hadn't spoken.

Lydia went from the kitchen into the deserted cafe and dialled Charlie on her mobile.

34

'There's a woman in my kitchen. Would you care to explain?'

'Lyds, sweetheart. I mean to call you first. Are you okay?'

Mollified by the concern in his tone, even while she knew it was carefully calculated, Lydia tried to hold onto her righteous anger. 'I'm not okay, no. You sent a cook. I don't need a cook because I'm not opening the cafe. You said I didn't have to run The Fork. You said –'

'Angel isn't a cook, she's an artist. You wait until you taste her pastries.'

Lydia rolled her eyes to heaven and prayed for strength. 'I'm not going to taste her pastries because she isn't going to be cooking any. I can't afford to pay anybody, to start a business. That's the only reason I'm living here. I'm broke.'

'I'm paying her,' Charlie said. 'You don't have to worry.'

'But you said I didn't have to run a business if I didn't want to, you said this was just a place to stay.'

'Lydia, Sweetheart. You know how it goes. I told you I needed the place to look used. What better way to do that than actually use it?'

Lydia closed her eyes. She hated it when her mother was right.

'So this place is opening?'

'On Saturday,' Charlie said. 'Don't worry. No publicity, no renovations, nobody will even come in.'

Lydia opened her eyes long enough to look through the grimy windows which faced the street. He was right, nobody in their right mind would walk into a place which looked like this to eat. Unless they knew it was owned by Charlie and they thought it was a front for something more interesting.

'How long do I have to open for?'

'A couple of weeks. Month, tops.'

'I won't be here for a month. I meant hours. How many during the day to make it look legit?'

'Whatever you like,' his voice was warm, now, happy that Lydia was cooperating. 'And I think it will be safer. After what happened I don't like the thought of you all alone in the building. If you've got people downstairs, even just Angel, it makes the place safer.'

Well that sounded good, Lydia had to admit. She sighed. 'What if I open for two hours a day, just mid-afternoon to miss the breakfast, lunch and after-work crowds? You can put whatever you like on the books.'

'Now you've got the idea,' Charlie said approvingly. 'Minimum hours. You can flip the sign whenever you like.'

'I appreciate your concern, but what else is this about? You don't really need to open the place, nobody official is going to bother you –' Lydia began, then she stopped, realising she didn't want to know. 'Never mind.'

'We can talk more in person. I'll be round soon.'

In the kitchen, Angel had rolled up her sleeves and was kneading dough.

'You don't need to do that,' Lydia said. 'I'm not opening today.' I'm not opening at all, she added silently. She wouldn't be here long enough for any of this nonsense and, once she was gone, Charlie could do what he liked.

'This is for the freezer,' Angel said without looking up. 'I need a stock ready.'

Lydia thought about telling her that she didn't need any stock ready as they wouldn't be selling any food anytime soon, but she decided life was too short and went back upstairs to put on some war paint. She knew she looked like shit and didn't want to present Charlie with the pale, wan visage she had seen in the mirror that morning. She might be currently persona-non-grata at her place of employment, she might have been attacked by an armed man the day before, but Lydia Crow was nobody's victim and she had no intention of looking like one. Especially not in front of the head of the Crow Family.

36

UNCLE CHARLIE SAT in the seat opposite, his hands on the Formica table, palms down. His shirt sleeves were rolled up exposing hairy forearms, the skin inked with old green and black tattoos. Lydia knew that the twisting vines continued up his arms and over his chest and stomach and that the Family emblem, the silhouette of a crow in flight, was repeated several times. When she had been little she had sat on his legs and traced the lines of ink. 'How many crows can you find?' Uncle Charlie had said and then bounced his legs up and down so that Lydia's vision had blurred and the ink had seemed to shift.

Angel brought a pot of coffee and poured it, her expression blank.

Charlie didn't speak, even after she had returned to the kitchen and Lydia decided to wait him out. She busied herself with the milk and then, on a whim, added a sachet of brown sugar to her drink. It was pleasant to stir the liquid and she counted the rotations rather than look at her silent uncle.

'I can't read you,' Charlie said finally.

'I'm an open book,' Lydia replied, forcing herself to look into Charlie's face.

He leaned back in his seat, clearly sizing her up. 'Little Lydia, all grown up.'

'You said you needed a favour. I'm assuming you're talking something in addition to this little set-up?' Lydia waved a hand to indicate The Fork. 'Are you going to send in a manager for that, or will it just be me and Angel.' Lydia mentally kicked herself. 'Angel on her own, I mean. I'm not managing anything.'

'I need an investigator.' Charlie said, his face and voice serious.

Was he making fun of her? There had to be hundreds in the city. Every single one of them more qualified.

'I can't use any of my regular crowd,' Charlie said, as if

37

reading her thoughts. 'This has to be very private.'

'That's in the job description. Any decent investigator is going to be completely discreet.' Quite apart from the fact that nobody in their right mind would screw over the Crows.

'I need someone I trust,' he said.

Lydia leaned back in her seat and resisted the urge to reply. He wasn't telling her anything that suggested he needed her, the lame duck of the Crow Family. He wanted her back in London and he still wasn't telling her why.

'I will pay your standard rate, of course.'

Lydia named her hourly rate. 'Plus expenses.'

He nodded. 'There's a bonus if you complete the job, too. I look after my people and I reward results.'

'And I stay here rent-free, hassle-free,' she put a little emphasis on the words, 'as arranged.'

He hesitated for a micro second and then nodded.

'Good,' Lydia said. 'So, what's the case?' Lydia didn't really believe there was one. Charlie was up to something else and she was just curious enough to play along until she found out what.

'Madeleine is missing.'

'My cousin, Maddie?' Lydia frowned. Family was sacred. Charlie wouldn't lie about that. 'For how long?'

'Five days,' Charlie said. 'I've followed every lead I can think of, checked with her friends and the people she works with. I've looked in all her usual locations, interviewed her ex-boyfriend.'

That wouldn't have been fun for the ex, Lydia thought. 'Is he still breathing?'

Charlie nodded, his expression perfectly neutral. 'He had nothing to do with it.'

The certainty of his words said it all. Charlie Crow knew how to conduct an interview.

'What about a current boyfriend? Anyone on the scene?'

'That's what I want you to find out.'

Lydia sat back, unconvinced. Charlie was all-powerful, head of the infamous Crow Family. Every single person he spoke to in connection with this would have spilled every last secret they had, every illicit thought they had ever had, every grudge they had held. He really didn't need her. She opened her mouth to say as much, but Charlie spoke first.

'I can't be on this,' Charlie said, lifting his massive shoulders. 'Not anymore. I'm like a hawk amongst the sparrows. It draws attention and this can't get out.'

The truth of that statement hit her even as she was saying 'I know'. It would look weak. A problem in the Family, the merest suggestion that someone had got to a Crow, that sort of thing had repercussions. None of the families had any real power, not like the good old days. The Crows had the most, though, and that mattered.

'Tristan Fox has been sniffing around. Either he senses something is wrong and he wants to press an advantage while I'm weak or he has something to do with it and he's gloating.'

Now Lydia was properly shocked. 'He wouldn't. He would never dare.'

'Things have changed,' Charlie said gently. 'You've been away a long time.'

'Five years,' Lydia said. And the truce had held for seventy-five before that. The thought that it might crack was unimaginable. Horrifying.

Charlie must have seen something in her face as his grim expression softened and, at once, he looked like the uncle she remembered. His hands had stayed completely still but now he moved, reaching across to cover her hand with one of his. It was massive, dwarfing hers. 'Nothing is going to happen. We won't let it. Tristan, me, David and Alejandro. None of us want that so it won't happen.'

Lydia swallowed hard, then nodded. 'I'll find Madeleine,'

she managed. 'I'm sure she's just taken a few days away. Her mum's a bit...' She stopped speaking, remembering abruptly that Madeleine's mum, Daisy, was Charlie's aunt.

'She is.' He smiled properly for the first time. 'That's another reason I want back-up.'

CHAPTER FOUR

Lydia's mum married into the Crow Family with her eyes wide open. When she met Lydia's dad, he was twenty-five and a big deal. Not as powerful as his big brother, Charlie, but a man to watch nonetheless. Mum was twenty-two and doing a PhD in biochemistry. She knew about the forces in the world, the building blocks of life and the tiny little pieces of matter which made up every single thing in the universe. She was an outsider, having grown up in Maidstone. She had heard rumours about the four Families, but had dismissed them as urban legend. She knew that only children believed in magic and that her beloved science explained everything in the physical world. And then she met Henry Crow in a bar and watched while he pulled coins from thin air, thinking that he was very good at sleight of hand.

Lydia had loved to hear the story of how they met, the idea of her suburban parents drinking cocktails in a bar and being smitten with each other across a crowded room, as quaint and alien as an old film. When she pictured the scene, it was practically in black-and-white.

'And then he sent flowers to the lab, even though I

41

hadn't told him where I worked. And waited outside for hours because he didn't know what time I would be finished.'

'Which was cute, not creepy,' Lydia would add, smiling to show she was joking and truly wasn't raining on her mother's good memory.

'And I just knew.' She always finished with this. This and a dreamy, faraway expression that was hard to decipher. It was happy, certainly, but mixed with other ingredients that a teenage Lydia hadn't recognised.

Susan Sykes had only one condition before she joined in holy matrimony; that if they had children, they would be brought up away from the Family and, as far as possible, away from magic. Henry Crow whole-heartedly agreed – Lydia's parents really were ridiculously well-suited and, when Susan was nearing her due date, they moved lock-stock out of Camberwell and Henry handed in his resignation to Grandpa Crow. Once Lydia was old enough, her dad explained that it hadn't been that easy and, if he had been the eldest son, it would have been impossible. Luckily, that role was inhabited by Charlie. Charlie didn't understand Henry's desire but he was a good big brother and he respected Henry's decision and he smoothed the path with Grandpa.

Standing on the pavement outside her parents' 1930s bay-fronted semi-detached on the quiet leafy street she had been desperate to escape, Lydia felt the familiar mix of love and guilt and panic. She didn't know why, but her childhood home made her skin itch, like it was a too-tight dress. Taking a job in Scotland had been about more than just finding her professional calling, it had also been about minimising contact with the two people who were, at this moment, pulling back the net curtain at the living room window and waving enthusiastically. And there was the volume knob on her guilt, twisted up to ten.

42

Her mother was already opening the front door. 'Darling!' Then, a small frown. 'You're too thin, are you eating?'

'All the time,' Lydia said, kissing her mum's soft cheek and hugging her tightly.

'Look who's here.' Susan was turning, her voice raised and unnaturally bright. It must be a bad day. Lydia braced herself, but her father stepped forward and hugged her, too.

'Lyds,' he said. 'My beautiful girl.'

Lydia blinked back sudden tears. 'Hi Dad, how are you doing?'

'We won the rugby,' he said, turning away and heading back towards the living room.

'Congratulations,' Lydia said, scanning his figure for weight loss and his movements for shakiness.

'Tea?' Her mum still sounded as if she'd been sucking helium and her cheeks were flushed.

'Sure,' Lydia changed course and led the way to the kitchen.

'Charlie phoned,' her mother said, the moment her feet crossed from the hall into the tiny square kitchen.

'Oh?' Lydia concentrated on filling the kettle, pulling cups from the little wooden mug tree and getting the milk out of the fridge. The longer she could put off looking at her mother, the longer she would have to formulate some kind of reassuring response.

'He says Madeleine has gone missing and that you are looking for her.'

'Mmm.' Lydia made a non-committal noise to hide her surprise. What was Charlie doing running to her parents, spreading the news? She held up the sugar jar. 'Still two for Dad? Or have the anti-sugar police knocked down the door, yet?'

'Is it true?'

'It's just a job,' Lydia said, keeping her eyes on the tea. 'You know I'm an investigator. Charlie wants my professional opinion.' She squeezed the teabag on the side of the mug and then put it into the pot her mother kept for the purpose.

'I told you there would be strings. You know how we feel about...' Her mother took a breath, tried again. 'It's not safe.'

'I'll be careful.' A stack of rinsed eggshells sat in a cardboard container, waiting to go out to the compost heap along with the used teabags and the sight of this familiar domestic detail, clutched her heart. Was her dad even tending his beloved compost heap anymore? 'How is Dad doing?' She asked, finally looking at her mum.

'Good days and bad days.' She picked up a cloth and began wiping up non-existent spills from the gleaming worktop. 'It's been better since –' She stopped abruptly and hung the cloth over the tap.

'Since I've been away.' Lydia finished her mother's sentence. Swallowing the bitter pill.

'Just coincidence, darling.' She reached out and patted Lydia's arm.

In the living room, Henry Crow was watching the snooker with the sound turned off. He accepted his mug of tea and then frowned at Lydia, as if trying to place her.

No, no, no. 'Enjoying the snooker, Dad?' It was just an excuse to use his name, to remind him of their relationship. Every time he forgot her it was like a blow.

'Yeah. It's all right.' He blew on his tea, the steam fogging up his glasses. 'How was the frozen north?'

Relief flooded through Lydia's body. 'Yeah. It's all right.' She smiled. 'Bit chilly.'

Her dad took his glasses off and squinted at her. His blue eyes were as bright as ever and his face still handsome. 'I don't like that job.'

'I know, Dad,' Lydia said. 'I do, though.'

'Too dangerous,' he said.

'Are you staying for dinner?' Her mum was perched on

44

the edge of the sofa, looking as if she wanted to get up again. She was never one for sitting still.

'Sure,' Lydia said. 'Thanks.'

'It's terrible about little Madeleine but you're not to get involved.'

'She's my cousin.'

'Second cousin. And she's Family. It'll be handled. Charlie will sort it.'

'He's asked me, though,' Lydia said. 'And I'm Family, too.'

Her mum hesitated then she said: 'I know, dear.'

'Who is missing?' Dad had his glasses back on but he must have cleaned them with his fingertips or a less-than-fresh handkerchief as they were smeared.

'Madeleine. Daisy and John's little girl.'

Daisy was her dad's cousin.

'Who the hell is John?'

Lydia wanted to close her eyes, to block out the sight of her Dad's confused expression.

'Daisy's husband,' her mum was saying. 'The accountant.'

'That bloody Pearlie.'

'Darling,' her mother shot a warning look. 'Don't say that. John is a very nice man and he's good to Daisy. You like him. He brought you that ale back from Somerset.'

'When did you last see them?' Lydia asked.

'Oh, couple of months. You know what we're like.'

Her parents loved their family and were loyal, but they kept away as much as possible.

'It was January I think. There was a pot luck at Charlie's and we missed the last one, so we thought we'd better...'

'Was Madeleine there?'

'Oh, yes. Looking very pretty, too. Not too thin the way some girls get.'

'And did she seem happy?'

'I don't know,' her mother looked mystified by the question. 'She was probably bored. You know what those

45

gatherings are like. All the old ones reliving their past glories.'

'Was she talking to her parents? All seem well there?'

'Oh, darling, I'm sorry,' her mother shook her head. 'I hardly said two words to the girl.'

AFTER STUFFING herself with her mother's delicious home-cooking, Lydia said goodbye to her father in the living room. The television was off, but he was staring at it anyway. Perhaps he was looking at his own reflection, or just deep in thought. At the door, Lydia kissed her mother. 'I'll keep in touch. I promise.'

'Come for lunch next weekend? If you're not too busy.' Her mother's ash blonde hair fell into two perfect curtains around her face and she had recently applied her habitual red lipstick. She was as beautiful as ever, but there were new lines on her brow and around her eyes. She looked worried.

'If I can,' Lydia said. 'I'll text you.'

Her mother made a face. 'Call me. I want to hear your voice.'

Lydia hugged her again.

'You know you can stay here,' her mother said, pulling back to look into Lydia's eyes. 'Your dad will cope.'

Lydia swallowed. 'It's fine. The Fork is fine. It's great.'

Her mother's worry lines deepened. 'What about your job in Scotland? I don't want you to lose that one.'

'I won't,' Lydia said, suddenly desperate to leave. This was the problem with parents. Their love was a weight. Reassuring and solid and necessary, but a weight none-theless.

THAT EVENING AT THE FORK, Lydia was alone in the café. She had raided the kitchen freezer and baked a couple of

46

Angel's pastries in the industrial-sized oven. If Charlie was going to insist on keeping a chef on the payroll, then Lydia was damned if she was going to buy and cook her own dinner. She had a bottle of beer to go with it and sat in the booth that she had sat in with Charlie earlier. She could still sense the faint residue of Crow from his seat. Either her senses were sharper here in London or it was testament to Charlie's strength.

A dark shape loomed in front of the plate glass in the café's front door and Lydia felt her heart lurch. For a moment she saw the shape as giant black bird. In that instant she could imagine the sharp curve of a beak, and the bedtime stories of the The Night Raven, mythical scourge of the Crow Family leaped into her mind. The shape moved, knocking loudly on the wooden frame of the door, and the illusion disappeared.

'Sorry to bother you, I was just passing and I saw the light was on.'

Detective Chief Inspector Fleet was wearing a grey wool three quarter length coat over a dark suit and there were droplets of water on his short black hair.

'What can I do for you officer?' Lydia said, annoyed with herself for being so fanciful and jumpy. Visiting her father always brought those old memories back, the stories of Crow magic and vengeful raven-shaped spirits. 'At this time of night,' she added.

He smiled as if they were sharing a joke.

'I wanted to check that you were okay. After yesterday.'

Yesterday. When an armed man had threatened her life. Lydia tried to think of an appropriate response. Something which encompassed everything she had felt, everything she was feeling. The exhilaration of a near-death experience and the intervention of a fully fledged ghost, the terror of the moment, and the strange wild freedom it had left, like unexpected cargo washed up on a beach. 'I'm fine,' she said.

Fleet was looking at her steadily. Like he was trying to work something out. Lydia wondered if this was a modern policing technique. Lull your suspect with weird friendliness and after-hours visits then, pow, hit them with an impromptu interrogation. She wasn't a suspect, though. She was a victim. Surely.

'I brought you a house-warming,' he lifted a bottle of red wine from a supermarket carrier bag.

'I thought you said you were just passing.'

'Okay,' Fleet said. 'I bought the wine to go with my dinner. That's why it's so beautifully gift-wrapped.' He smiled again, his eyes warm and crinkly, and Lydia wondered what it took to make a person that easy in their own skin. 'Still, it's on offer…'

Lydia hesitated, weighing up her options and the chances of the detective just buggering off again. Finally, figuring that a police contact was a useful thing to cultivate and that she was curious enough to know what he wanted. She retreated to the cafe counter and began searching for appropriate glasses. There were squat heavy tumblers which were probably used for juice and she wiped them over with a tea towel.

After she unscrewed the bottle and poured, putting one glass in front of the detective, she sat opposite him.

He raised his glass in a brief salute and then drank, looking around the room as if searching for something. 'This place still looks great,' he said after a moment. 'Bit of a clean-up and it would be good as new.'

'It's not mine,' Lydia said, wondering when he would get to the reason for his visit. 'And I'm not staying long,' Lydia didn't know why she mentioned that, it wasn't as if it was any of his business.

'Because of the break-in?'

'No,' Lydia said. 'Because I don't want to run a cafe. I'm

just staying here for a few weeks, until I sort out something better.'

'Your uncle still own it? Charles Crow?'

Lydia took a sip of her wine, watching DCI Fleet over the rim of the glass. 'Just passing, eh? Got something you want to ask me, officer?'

'Just making conversation,' he said.

'You said you grew up around here, used to come in this place with your aunt?'

'That's right,' the warmth was back, he really did have good memories.

'Well, you know that there's no such thing as a casual question about Charles Crow, then, don't you?'

He put down his glass. 'I apologise.'

Lydia downed the rest of her wine. 'You'd better go.'

'It's my job to ask questions,' he said, finishing his drink. 'And it's my job to protect people, too.' He leaned forward suddenly and took Lydia's hand. 'Do you need protecting?'

Lydia stared at his enormous hand, completing enveloping her own. It was warm and dry and not at all unpleasant. Lydia forced herself to pull her hand away and he let go instantly.

'I'm fine, thank you for asking,' she said.

He stood up, then, and Lydia reminded herself that she was pleased. Instead of heading toward the front door, though, he swivelled and walked to the back of the cafe and behind the counter, pushing through the swing door to the kitchen before Lydia could react. 'Hey,' she said, following him. 'You can't go back there.'

He was stood in the middle of the kitchen, looking around with the same intensity.

'You can't be back here,' Lydia said. 'Not without a warrant.'

'Now you sound like your uncle,' DCI Fleet said.

'I don't know what you're looking for but I can assure

you this place has been deserted for years, there's nothing exciting here.'

'Oh, I don't know.' The detective gave Lydia a long slow look that made her heart kick up. It wasn't a professional look, it was a challenge and Lydia squared her shoulders and forced herself to meet his gaze.

'Is this the new way the crooked cops collect kickbacks around here?'

He looked shocked and then guilty. 'This is a personal visit, didn't I make that clear?' He moved back, hands in the air. 'I can see I made a mistake, and for that I apologise. I'll leave you in peace.'

Lydia walked him to the front door, trying to reconcile the swift change from wolf to sheep.

'Good night, Ms Crow.'

Lydia shut the door and bolted it, certain of one thing: there was no way DCI Fleet had called by to hit on her, and his sudden retreat had nothing to do with her calling out his odd behaviour. He came looking for something and either he decided it wasn't here or he found it. Lydia looked around at the empty cafe and tried to see what Fleet might have seen. After a few minutes she gave up trying to read the mind of a copper and went to bed. She would find Maddie and then get back to her real life. It didn't matter what DCI Fleet thought he knew about her.

CHAPTER FIVE

Lydia knew that Uncle Charlie had connections to investigators, heavies and probably flexibly-minded officers of the law, too; he didn't need her services. She also couldn't believe that Madeleine was really missing, that there wasn't some other angle that Charlie knew about. It was inconceivable that he would be setting her, known damp squib, in sole charge of the investigation if there was a chance that Maddie was truly in trouble. It was a given that Charlie must have at least one ulterior motive for the charade and Lydia thought it fair to assume it was probably to do with drawing her into the Family business. Henry Crow's refusal to continue Grandpa Crow's legacy and to bring up his only child away from Camberwell had not been a universally popular decision.

On the other hand, Lydia was on an unpaid sabbatical that she couldn't afford and any job which kept her away from Aberdeen, even a bogus one for her terrifying uncle, was better than nothing. Lydia explained all of this while Emma listened, deftly cutting up carrot and cucumber into sticks, slicing cheese and putting out snack-plates for the kids. 'What happened in Aberdeen?'

51

Lydia looked meaningfully at the children, their soft-haired heads bent over a bright green lump of plastic with a screen which was emitting random noises and the occasional 'good job!' in a perky American voice.

'Put that down and have some food,' Emma said. 'You can finish the puzzle after.'

The device made a thunk sound when they dropped it and scrambled to their seats.

'It's complicated,' Lydia said, wondering how much she could safely say in front of the children.

'Did you do a mistaking?' Archie surprised Lydia with his question – she hadn't thought he was paying attention. He had a dollop of houmous on his chin and three carrot sticks clutched in one hand.

'No,' Lydia said. 'But I annoyed somebody.'

'How?' Archie said, thoughtfully scooping chin-houmous into his mouth.

'Um,' Lydia tried to think of an appropriate version of the story and then gave up, defeated.

'Did you bonk them on the nose?' Archie said, not ready to let the subject go.

'Hang on,' Lydia said, 'what's this?' She leaned across the kitchen table and plucked a coin from behind Archie's ear.

His eyes widened as she put the coin into his hand and Maisie squealed loud enough to pierce an eardrum. 'My have!'

'Yes,' Lydia, said. Mock serious. 'But you must sit very, very still and very, very quietly.' Maisie instantly stopped wriggling and became still as a piece of rock. A piece of rock that clearly wanted to squeal. Lydia reached out, feeling clumsily around Maisie's right ear. 'No, nothing here, that's strange...' Maisie's face was a picture of excitement and anticipation, just as it began to falter into uncertainty, Lydia switched to Maisie's left ear. 'Oh! Here we go!' She produced a gold coin and gave it to Maisie.

52

'One day you're going to have to tell me how you do that,' Emma said.

'Sleight of hand,' Lydia said breezily. 'Years of practice.'

Later, once the kids had finished their snack and had run through to the living room for television-time, Lydia washed up the plates and cups while Emma wiped down the table. Then, she reached into the fridge and brought out the bottle of white wine she had brought round and stashed there earlier.

Emma's face lit up. 'You always have the best ideas.'

'Hold that thought,' Lydia said, pouring them both a glass and taking a large gulp. She loved Maisie and Archie, but three hours of their company and she was exhausted. She had no idea how Emma did it.

'Okay. So, one of the guys I was following wasn't too pleased with the evidence I gathered. He made some threats.'

'How did he know it was you?'

Lydia slugged some wine. 'His wife.'

'She was the person who hired you in the first place?'

Lydia nodded. 'Uh-huh.'

'Charming.'

'She was all set for a lucrative divorce but he talked her round. Apparently all is romantic bliss once again. It happens.' Not often, in Lydia's limited experience as a private eye, but there were bound to be exceptions.

'She came to you to get evidence that he was cheating?'

Lydia nodded. 'She knew what he was up to, or pretty much at any rate, but she wanted hard evidence. Said he would weasel his way out of it, come up with excuses and she didn't want to waver.' Lydia could picture the woman sitting in the office, her hair perfectly styled and her eyes dry. Lydia had thought that she was past the worst of it, had reached some sort of acceptance, not like some of the poor buggers who were red-eyed and hopeful. Worried that their husband or boyfriend was lying to them, but also hoping that Lydia report back that they were actually helping out at a local cat shelter or something. Mrs Carter had been different, though, and Lydia would have laid money that she would take the surveillance report and use it to beat up Mr Carter in court. Which just went to show how much Lydia knew about marriage. And that gambling was a bad idea. 'Apparently now they are going to renew their vows on a beach in St Lucia. I just thought it would be a good idea to make myself scarce until they go away. By the time they come back, all loved up and renewed, hopefully the thirst for vengeance will have died down.'

'I don't understand –' Emma began, then she said: 'I guess your evidence wasn't clear enough and he still talked his way out of it.'

'It was clear,' Lydia said, thinking of the explicit photographs and the twenty-second video. Longest twenty seconds of her life.

'Bloody hell,' Emma said. 'Nice job you got yourself. Ever thought about a change of career?'

Lydia thought she had managed a smile, but the tiredness and the wine must have made it go wonky.

'Sorry. Just joking, Lyds.' Emma looked stricken. 'What's wrong?'

Lydia took a deep breath and told Emma about her unwanted visitor.

She was gratifyingly shocked and concerned and it made Lydia feel a thousand times better to talk it out. She finished with a detailed description of the hot cop, but Emma was stuck on the intruder.

'He had a gun? Jesus H.'

'I know,' Lydia drained her glass and poured another one, topping up Emma's at the same time.

'And he just collapsed and fell over the railing?'

'It was weird,' Lydia avoided answering the question

directly, wanting to minimise the lies she told her best friend, while avoiding the tricky subject of a full-on poltergeist. Emma was her normal friend. Her one chance at a normal life and she wasn't about to destroy it.

'Your life is mental,' Emma shook her head.

Okay. Normal-ish life.

'I can't believe you didn't lead with that. An armed robbery on your first night back in London. What are the bloody chances?'

Lydia paused, her glass halfway to her lips. It was a good point. She hadn't told anybody in Aberdeen where she was going, but that was no guarantee. Phones were traceable, she could have been followed...

'What are you thinking?' Emma was looking worried.

'Just wondering if it was a coincidence. If not, then the guy is either connected to my work up north or to the Family. I mean, I didn't recognise him, but I was very scared, so maybe I had face-blindness or something.'

'I don't like the sound of either of those options,' Emma said.

'Me neither.'

LYDIA GOT the train back into Camberwell, pleasantly buzzed from the wine and the chat with Emma. As she walked back from the station toward the cafe, she took stock of her situation. One of the plus sides to not being magical, was that Lydia had always applied herself in other areas. She had worked hard at school and excelled until it had all seemed pointless. She knew she wasn't going to go to university so she started doing the bare minimum. Then she had thrown herself into learning a practical skill. She had started to train as an electrician, thinking that she could work with a different kind of power, but it had all been diagrams and safety talks and it had left her feeling more helpless than ever. After half-heartedly working as a waitress, an accounts assistant and a dog-groomer, she had turned to work as a PI with something approaching desperation. With no clue as to what she wanted to do, only the certainty that she hadn't found her calling in the back room of 'Pretty Paws' she had been toying between long-distance truck driver and private investigator, and had made the decision with a coin toss.

One year later and she had just been finding her feet, starting to feel as if she wasn't making stupid mistakes all the bloody time when the little situation with Mr and Mrs Carter blew-up. It didn't feel fair. If there was such a thing as a Career Fairy, she wasn't sprinkling any of her magic over Lydia.

Climbing the stairs to the exit at Denmark Hill station and joining the fume-filled street, Lydia decided to call her boss. She couldn't put it off any longer and, besides, she had read somewhere that standing to make a phone call helped you to be more assertive on the line. Right now, Lydia felt as if she needed every advantage she could muster, so she tucked under the cover of a bus stop, straightened her shoulders and pressed the call button. Karen picked up almost immediately. 'It's Lydia,' she said, aware that she was using a new phone and Karen wouldn't have her number.

'You're being cautious?' Karen said.

'Of course,' Lydia replied, offended.

'It's all been quiet here,' Karen said. 'Nothing doing.'

That was a relief. Unless it meant that the action had simply followed her to London.

'How are you?' Karen wasn't one for touchy-feeling emotional conversations, so Lydia knew this was a business query.

'Two weeks ought to do it and then I'll be back.'

'Good. I can't hold the position for longer than that.'

'I understand,' Lydia said. It was expected, but Lydia still felt her heart sink to her stomach. Two weeks wasn't long. Worse still, she knew that if she had failed to find Madeleine alive and well a damn-sight earlier, losing her job was going to be the least of her worries. If her suspicions about this being a set-up weren't true and somebody really had messed with Madeleine Crow, outright war in London was a distinct possibility.

LYDIA PASSED her boat-like Volvo when she was still three streets away from the cafe. It had been the closest she had been able to park and she gave it a cursory check as she walked by. Even if she hadn't had wine, she felt no desire to drive it around to look for a closer space. It wasn't worth the hassle.

Well Street, imaginatively named back when Camberwell was still clinging to its roots as a sleepy village, was a typical London thoroughfare. Victorian and Georgian architecture brooded above the plate glass windows of the betting shops and hairdressers. There was a nice-looking pub which had obviously had the full modern refurb and gastro-food makeover, a newsagent, and even an honest-to-god hardware store which seemed to sell everything from screws to hair extensions. There was a branch of the Silver's firm in Camberwell but, naturally, the office was on the fanciest street in the borough, its windows overlooking the park.

Lydia hadn't meant to stop, but the fruit outside the grocer looked so shiny and appetising that she suddenly had a craving for something sweet and juicy and wholesome. She was more familiar with cravings for fatty goodness or the promise of alcoholic mind-shut-up potion, so was taken by surprise. The shelves outside the glass window of the shop were beautifully presented with punnets of strawberries, apricots, grapes and plums nestled on bright plastic grass and little chalkboards with the prices. Still, it usually took more than a bit of Instagram-worthy styling to make Lydia want to ingest vitamins and, the closer she looked, the more she could see that there was something special about the fruit. It wasn't just delicious-looking, it was downright tempting.

Inside the shop the smell was intoxicating. Fresh. Sweet. Good. Sharp citrus mingled with tropical and apple notes and Lydia felt an overwhelming urge to pick up one of the handy wicker baskets piled at the entrance and fill it to the brim. She wanted to pick up one of the gigantic white peaches and sink her teeth right into it, could imagine the juice running down her throat so vividly that it was as if it had already happened. She realised that she was standing stock-still in the middle of the room, her eyes shut and she forced them open. She had a peach in her hand, an inch from her lips. The fuzz of the skin felt like the finest fabric she had ever touched and the colour the most beautiful thing she had ever seen.

Something was definitely up. She deliberately moved the peach away from her mouth and, with an effort of will, put it down.

Lydia was being watched. There wasn't a traditional shop counter, just a till next to a weighing machine on a high round table, like the kind you got in a bar. Next to it was a teenage girl perched on a stool, which also looked like it had been nicked from a nightclub. The girl had glossy black hair which was swept to one side in a low ponytail. Her eyes were heavily-lined in Kohl, making the whites of her eyes startling.

'I like your shop,' Lydia said. It wasn't what she had intended to say, but she was finding it increasingly difficult to think. The urge to sink her teeth into a peach or a plum or bite into a crunchy apple was crowding everything else out.

The girl didn't smile but she inclined her head slightly.

That's when Lydia saw it and everything fell into place. A shining pearl was fixed in the second piercing of her left ear. Lydia had walked right into a shop owned by a Pearl. No wonder she wanted to buy the whole lot.

She nodded and smiled, not wanting to be rude, and then backed out of the door. The produce was still calling to her, still making her mouth water and her insides contract with hunger, but now that her brain was engaged, the veil had lifted slightly. Enough, anyway, to give her motor control of her feet and creep her way out onto the street.

Lydia didn't stop moving until she was several shop fronts away and, even then, she didn't dare look back. She made a mental note never to pass so closely again, to cross the road at that point and not to look at the fruit displayed on the pavement. She couldn't believe how intense the effect had been. When had the Pearls got so strong?

CHAPTER SIX

Back at The Fork, Lydia side-stepped a crate of cleaning supplies which had mysteriously materialised next to the door to the stairs, and headed up to the flat. She had brought in her bags and suitcase from the car before going to Emma's but before unpacking, she went through the rooms, looking for the ghost. 'Hello? If you are here don't pop up behind me or something. I'm not in the mood.' She waited a beat. Nothing.

After organising her stuff, Lydia went online to check out Madeleine's social media. She had a Facebook page but, like most nineteen year olds, didn't seem to use it very much. There were pictures of her with her friends, arms around each other's necks or holding up their fingers to their faces. She had been tagged in a beach-shot in Ibiza with the caption 'St A crew chilling'. The picture showed a group of bronzed and lovely girls in bikinis and St A referred to St Anne's, Madeleine's former private girls' school. Madeleine wasn't looking at the camera and smiling, but instead looked away, at something out of shot, and it gave her a whimsical, thoughtful appearance. Was that the image of a girl who had run away from home? A girl who was planning a great escape?

Could you even run away from home at nineteen? Lydia imagined, for a moment, telling the police. 'And the woman is nineteen? And she's been out of contact with her family for one week?' A beat. 'Are you on crack?' In imagining 'the police' the image of Fleet had come to mind and it was his voice that was heavily laden with sarcasm as it asked why she was panicking over a grown woman not being in touch with her parents for seven days. He was asking all of this in his delicious, deep voice. It was rather... Pleasant. *Get a grip, Lydia.*

Lydia threatened herself with a cold shower and returned to the screen to resume cyberstalking her second cousin. Madeleine didn't appear to be on Twitter at least, not under her own name, and her Snapchat was only available to accepted friends. Lydia sent a request with the message 'hey cuz'. Her Instagram hadn't been updated since last week. Madeleine's last post was an arty shot of a couple of tall glasses filled with sparkling clear liquid, dotted with red pomegranate seeds. The hashtags included #adultdrinks #adulting and #cocktailfun.

Lydia squinted at the picture for a while, trying to work out whether there was anything in the picture which identified the bar before realising that one of the hashtags actually gave the location. #Foxy. She scrolled back through Madeleine's pictures until she found one of a box of matches with gold embossed letters spelling Club Foxy underneath a logo which showed a stylised outline of a foxes head. Lydia's relief that it didn't look like the logo of a strip club (in Aberdeen, the word 'foxy' would definitely indicate women dancing sadly on podiums wearing micro shorts if not a full-out brothel) was suddenly and unpleasantly replaced by the realisation that should have come first... Club Foxy might have links to the Fox Family. It would be a brave business-owner in Camberwell who named their establishment 'Foxy' if they weren't cuddled up with the Family. 'Bollocks.'

'Language,' the ghost appeared next to the sofa, making Lydia's heart leap.

'You are going to give me a heart attack if you keep popping up like that.'

'So-rree,' the ghost said petulantly, hands on hips. 'I was talking for ages. It's not my fault you didn't hear me.'

'You've been there for ages?' Lydia tried not to feel creeped out and failed.

Ghost-boy nodded and the motion made Lydia want to throw up.

'What's bollocks, anyway?' He moved behind the sofa and leaned down to look at her laptop screen.

Lydia clicked to close the browser window and then wondered why she had bothered. Secrecy was such an ingrained habit, but who was he going to tell? His ghost pals? 'Do you speak to other people?'

'I told you, no one else can see me.'

'No. I mean –' Lydia stopped herself from saying 'dead people'. That seemed harsh. 'Other spirits.'

The ghost moved through the sofa and then arranged himself in a sitting position next to Lydia. He placed his hands carefully onto his knees, keeping his gaze dipped. Just when Lydia though he wasn't going to answer, he said: 'I haven't spoken to anyone since I died.'

Well, that sucked. 'I'm sorry,' Lydia said.

He glanced at her and she could see his eyes glistening with unshed tears. He wiped a hand across his face and sniffed.

'I'm trying to find my second cousin. She's nineteen and hasn't been seen by friends or family for a week.'

Ghost-boy perked up. 'You think she's dead?'

'No!' Being a ghost really messed with your sense of

propriety. Or he had always been insensitive. Murderous and insensitive. Suddenly it didn't seem like the best combo, and Lydia wondered if she ought to make more of an effort to be friendly. She re-opened the browser window and angled the screen towards him. 'I'm checking to see what she was doing before she disappeared and I found this picture.'

Lydia felt the ghost lean closer and the air temperature dropped a couple of degrees. 'She was clubbing?'

'Looks like,' Lydia said. 'Which isn't exactly shocking. It's just…'

The ghost was frowning at the screen. 'Foxy? That sounds a bit –'

'Indeed,' Lydia cut across him. 'I'm guessing that when Uncle Charlie called Madeleine's pals they wouldn't have been in too big a hurry to tell him where they had all been partying.'

He whistled and it sent a shiver that started at Lydia's scalp and ran over every inch of her skin. She grimaced.

'What?' The ghost leaned closer, his face getting more strange and inhuman. 'I can't help sounding this way. Don't you think I would prefer *not* to be dead?'

'Sure, but I'd prefer not to be haunted. At least you can move out. Which is something I would strongly advise. I don't need an undead flatmate. I need peace and quiet and not to be given a heart attack anytime soon.'

The ghost moved back, his face a picture of hurt. Eventually, he said: 'It's called 'moving on', you know.'

Lydia tried, and failed, to stamp down on her irritation. 'I don't care what you call it as long as you vacate my house.'

'One, it's not your house,' he held up one finger. 'Two, it's not a house,' he held up a second digit. 'And three, I'm not going anywhere.'

'This must be what it's like to have an annoying little brother,' Lydia said. 'Thank Christ I'm an only child.'

'This must be what it's like to finally have a living human being to communicate with after thirty lonely years, only to find out they are a total dick.' And then he disappeared which was a pretty cowardly way to finish an argument.

LYDIA WOKE up in the bare bedroom and threw one arm out automatically for her phone. No messages. She scrolled through her emails while lying down. One had come through at 8.15am from Karen, letting her know that she was no longer the named contact for the oil company which kept the firm on retainer. It made sense, Lydia wasn't in the office or available, after all, but it still stung. Karen had taken her on for work experience and then taken her on the following week. She had trained her and paid for the BTEC exam. Lydia had really thought she had found her place in the world.

And now here she was. In the forbidden land of Camberwell, site of tense family gatherings and stolen nights out as a rebellious teen. In Camberwell and doing a job for Uncle Charlie. A job in which she felt increasingly out of her depth. She had felt pretty good about her growing investigative skills, had even successfully completed a couple of small jobs on her own, but she had had the backing of the firm and Karen's guidance. She wasn't sure she was ready to be out on her own. She had thought that Charlie was making up a reason for her to come to London, not that there was a real problem to solve.

A cold stone of worry settled in Lydia's stomach as she considered the possibility. What if Madeleine really was in trouble? It was almost eight days, now, since anybody had heard from her and, a quick check online confirmed, she still hadn't popped up on any of her social media profiles. She knew that Charlie was persuasive but she was amazed that Madeleine's parents, her aunt Daisy and uncle John, hadn't insisted on calling the police.

She pulled on her favourite skinny jeans, a silky black top with a wide neck and added red lipstick. Grabbing her leather jacket, she headed downstairs and out through the cafe. It was mercifully empty but the smell of bleach was still thick in the air.

As Lydia locked the front door, she saw the ghost appear behind the glass. His face was pale like something at the bottom of a pool of water. He waved mournfully and Lydia felt absurdly bad for not shouting 'goodbye' to him. She raised a hand and mouthed 'see you later'. It was official: Living at The Fork had made her lose the plot.

Lydia knew that she must have been to her Aunt Daisy and Uncle John's house at some point during her childhood. The Crows all lived around Camberwell, apart from her own rebellious parents and the occasional ousted member who, sensibly enough moved far, far, away, and they had regular family events. Pot luck suppers, Christmas parties, New Year's Eve parties, summer BBQs, gigantic birthday parties for their children. If it wasn't for the magic and crime, they were like a supermarket advert. The odds were good that Lydia had climbed these front steps, clutching a parental hand and a wrapped gift, but ringing the doorbell now she couldn't remember it.

She did remember the woman who opened the door, though. Aunt Daisy had always been perfectly presented with immaculate makeup and styled hair and the kind of house you definitely had to take your shoes off to enter. She looked exactly the same as Lydia's memory, albeit ten years older. It hadn't been that long, but worry had etched the lines in her face more deeply and all the makeup in the

66

world couldn't cover the shadows under her eyes or the red rims where she had obviously just been crying.

'Lydia! Charles said you'd be visiting. Come in.'

The house which Madeleine had so recently vacated was a beautiful Georgian terrace with high ceilings, original features and all of the accoutrements of middle-class life. A range cooker in the large kitchen extension, with a big glass door which looked out onto decking complete with expensive-looking rattan furniture in slate grey.

Daisy moved around the kitchen, gathering glasses and sparkling water from the fridge. She retrieved a lemon from a bowl on the counter and cut a couple of slices. She paused. 'Did I ask you what you wanted?'

She hadn't but Lydia nodded. 'That looks great, thank you.'

'John's in his office.' Her lips pressed inward as if she were suppressing words.

'At home?'

She nodded. 'He says he has to keep working. I don't know how he can.' She put the glasses onto the big dining table and sat next to Lydia. Seeming to remember that she was speaking to little Lydia, her cousin's girl, she plastered on a simile of a smile. 'Don't mind me. Tell me all your news.'

Lydia took a sip of the cold water and then got out her notebook and pencil. 'I'm here to help.'

Daisy blinked.

Lydia wondered how much Charlie had, in fact, said. 'I've been working as an investigator, up in Scotland. I heard about Madeleine and came back to help.' Not strictly true, but anything to soften her up. Lydia hated the thought, the cold sergeant major she remembered was no longer in residence. Her formidable Aunt Daisy had been tenderised by fear for her beloved child.

'I knew you were in Scotland,' Daisy said. 'I didn't know you were doing that.'

Her tone made it sound like hooking. Lydia reminded herself that Daisy was stressed to the max and couldn't help herself. Probably. 'Can I ask you about Madeleine?'

Daisy looked at the table. 'Of course. If you think it will help. I told Charlie it was time to get the police involved, but he doesn't seem to think it would do any good. I think he's being pessimistic, they have all kinds of ways, now. Technology and so on.'

'He's asked me to help,' Lydia said. 'And he's right about the police. Madeleine is nineteen which means she is legally classed as an adult. Unless you have reason to believe she is at risk, or a danger to herself or others, then she would be classed as low or medium risk, which means low priority.'

'Not for us,' Daisy straightened. 'Our family still has clout, they would have to do something. There are old agreements –'

'Maybe,' Lydia said. 'And if I don't make any progress in a day or so, I will advise Charlie to contact the police.'

Daisy was clearly mollified by Lydia's serious tone and the prospect of an ally in her argument with Charlie. Lydia took out her notebook and flipped it open to a new page. 'Right. Just a few details, if you don't mind?'

Her aunt waved a hand, looking simultaneously disbelieving and hopeful.

'How did she seem. The last time you saw her.'

Daisy's shrug was more a convulsion. 'Same as usual. Happy.'

'You two were getting on well.'

'Naturally,' Daisy said. 'She has grown into a wonderful young woman. We'd had a few bad months here and there when she was younger, the usual teenage stuff, but nothing bad has happened for ages.'

Lydia made a note in her book, then asked. 'Can you remember what she was wearing the last time you saw her?'

Daisy's eyes widened and Lydia wondered if it was because Charlie had asked the same thing or whether she was surprised that he hadn't. 'I'm not sure.' Daisy closed her eyes. 'She was dressed for work. Pale grey trouser suit. Her linen one.'

'Did she have a bag? Her mobile phone?'

Daisy smiled. 'Of course she had her phone. Maddie doesn't even go to the bathroom without it.'

'iPhone?' Lydia said. 'I assume you've checked the Find My Phone app?'

'Charlie did,' Daisy said, looking suddenly vague. 'He said it wasn't working. Either she had switched off her GPS or the phone was broken or something.'

'So, it was the morning before she went to work? Can you tell me about her job?'

'At Minty PR.' Daisy looked away. 'To be honest, it wasn't all she had hoped for. Making tea and stapling things together as far as I could tell. I told her she had to start at the bottom, pay her dues, and that she would be given more responsibility later, but I know she was disappointed.'

'And friends? How are things going there?'

'Fine, I think.'

'All right,' Lydia had seen Karen pose the following questions a number of times and she was always direct about them. Perhaps easier to do when it wasn't your aunt across the table. Lydia swallowed before launching in. 'Forgive me for asking this, but has Madeleine made any new friends recently or started going to new places?'

Daisy frowned. 'Not that I know of.'

'How about a change in mood recently? Or behaviour? Has she been withdrawn or seemed ill or tired?'

'She was a bit tired after work sometimes.'

69

Okay, too subtle. Out with it, Lyds. 'Has she been doing drugs?'

The gleam of magic that Lydia could see as clearly as most people would see her Boden clothing was shimmering like an electric current through water. Lydia instinctively pushed her chair back, ready to run.

'No.' Daisy said eventually, her voice surprisingly even. 'She would never be so stupid.'

Lydia made a mark in her notebook, trying to convey how routine and normal these intrusive questions were. 'Gambling?'

'No.'

'Boyfriend or girlfriend?'

'Charles asked me that already.' Daisy's tone was less even, now.

'And what did you say?'

Daisy gave her a shocked look. It was fair enough; the last time they had seen each other, Lydia had been an almost-silent girl about the age her daughter was now. Now she was asking impertinent questions about her beloved baby girl. Lydia attempted a conciliatory tone. 'I need to get as much information as possible so that I can find Madeleine. I'm not trying to offend you and I know it might feel a bit strange, talking to me about these things, but I assure you I am a professional.'

'It's fine,' Daisy interrupted. 'I just don't have anything to add. Madeleine isn't in a relationship, she doesn't seem at all interested to be honest. Says she wants to establish her career. Actually,' Daisy pursed her lips for a second and then dived ahead. 'The actual words she used were 'I don't want to end up like you.' Meaning me.'

'I'm sure she didn't mean that,' Lydia said, ducking her head and writing 'unhappy at home?' in her notebook.

'I have no doubt that she did.' Daisy wiped underneath her eyes with her finger, although they appeared perfectly

70

dry. 'She never misses a moment to tell me how sad and boring and unenlightened my choices have been. Never mind that it meant she had a loving mother always at home, doing her every bidding.'

Lydia shut her notebook. 'May I use your bathroom?'

Daisy blinked. 'Of course. Upstairs on the right.'

'And I should say hello to Uncle John, too.'

'His study is third floor, directly ahead. Do knock first.'

'Right-oh.'

Having established a reason to take a long time, Lydia escaped upstairs. The first couple of doors she tried were the bathroom and a laundry cupboard but the third struck gold. It was clearly Madeleine's room as it had the unmistakeable vibe of a teenage girl. Layers of girlhood were visible, with a few precious soft toys (no longer on the bed, of course, but tucked on the bookshelf as if guarding the reading material), and a dressing table overflowing with both colourful canisters of body spray and heavy glass bottles of designer perfume.

There were clothes over the floor and piled in a heap on a chair in one corner. A swift examination under the bed and between the mattress and box-frame, revealed nothing except the fact that somebody was very diligent about vacuuming underneath the furniture. The walk-in closet revealed yet more clothes and a shoe collection lovingly catalogued in boxes with photographs attached to the outside. This beautiful Martha Stewart-worthy display was accessorised with a tangled pile of trainers, pumps and stilettos on the floor beneath the shelving.

There was a laptop on the desk and Lydia tried not to feel too envious as she noted the make and model. She lifted the lid and crossed her fingers that Madeleine was as half-arsed about internet security as she was about tidying her clothes. No password to get into the home screen and, bingo, when Lydia opened the browser and began typing the name of the first email client which sprang to mind, the auto-text finished it for her. She hit 'go' and Madeleine's email inbox appeared. She scanned the page, noting down the names of Madeleine's most common correspondents. The most recent emails were all from friends asking 'you okay, hon?' and variations. Lydia looked for the most recent email which had the 'replied' symbol next to it and clicked.

Hi Madeleine.
I'm sorry things haven't worked out here and I don't agree with the way in which it was handled. You will be missed around the office and I just wanted to wish you all the best.
If you want to get a coffee sometime, I would love to stay in touch.
Best wishes,
Verity

The email had been sent three weeks ago. Madeleine's reply was sent on the fifteenth. Her last morning in this bedroom.

Hi Verity,
I've been thinking about it all a lot and it would be good to talk.
Are you free today?
I'll be in town this afternoon. Call me!
Maddie

LYDIA FORWARDED the message to her own email. It would leave a footprint, she knew, but she just crossed her fingers that it wouldn't matter. What was a little invasion of privacy when measured against finding their daughter?

The sound of a toilet flushing down the hall made Lydia straighten involuntarily. She closed the browser window and shut the lid of the laptop. Pocketing her notebook, she moved swiftly to the door, just in time to hear a door open and close and footsteps coming closer. She held her breath while the footsteps continued, past the door. Please go back to your office, Lydia silently prayed to John. After a few seconds of silence, she opened the door. Her Uncle John was on the landing, one foot on the stairs which led to the third floor. Lydia moved as quickly as possible, plastering on a smile of greeting and hoping he hadn't caught which room she had emerged from.

'Lydia? I didn't know you were here.'

'It's good to see you,' Lydia said. 'How are you bearing up?'

A shadow passed across John's face. 'Fine. Fine. You know.'

Lydia nodded.

'What are you doing?'

'Visiting. I'm back from Scotland for a couple of weeks and Uncle Charlie asked me to help out with Maddie.'

The shadow became a storm and then, just as quickly, his face slackened and the emotion was wiped away. 'Madeleine is being very selfish. As usual.'

John looked behind Lydia. 'But what are you doing up here?'

'Bathroom,' Lydia said, remembering as she spoke that John had just come from there. 'Looking for the bathroom,' she amended.

'Right. Yes. This way.' Lydia had forgotten that John had always been clipped and formal. As a kid she had found it intimating but now she wondered if it meant he had never felt comfortable at the big family gatherings. After what her dad had said, she wondered if John's family background had prevented him from feeling properly at home with the Crows. Lydia was trying very hard not to use her own ability, weak though it was, in an attempt not to give out any stronger 'Crow vibes' than absolutely necessary. She had no idea whether other people could sense powers in the way that she could but since everybody else in the families were stronger than her, she didn't want to make assumptions to the contrary. Despite her best efforts, though, she could taste something hard and chalky in the air and see a faint pearlescent shimmer on John's skin.

'Well. Good to see you,' John said, turning away.

'What did you mean by selfish? Where do you think she is?'

John paused on the stairs, but didn't look at Lydia. He stared, instead, at the carpet. 'I don't know, but it will be exactly where she wants to be. And I don't think she will waste a moment worrying about the hell she is putting her mother through.'

Downstairs, Daisy was still sitting at the table, exactly as she had been. 'I'd better get going,' Lydia said. 'Thank you for the drink.'

Daisy nodded. 'Did you see John?'

'Uh-huh,' Lydia replied. 'He seems...' Lydia trailed off, unable to think of a polite way of saying 'sociopathic'.

'It's a coping mechanism,' Daisy said. Her face twisted, a sudden reveal of the pain she was feeling inside. 'At least, that's what I'm telling myself.'

'Well, it must be very hard...' She wondered how to phrase the question. 'Were they on good terms? Madeleine and her dad, I mean?'

'I told you,' Daisy said. 'We had the usual teenage blow ups, but nothing for ages. Everything was fine. Settled.'

Lydia nodded. 'Got it. Right. Thanks.' Christ, she had caught staccato speech from John.

'Well,' Daisy said, seemingly energised and back to her polite hostess mode. 'It's nice to see you. I hope you're spending plenty of time with your poor parents.'

'Um... Yes.' Poor parents?

'You broke your mother's heart, you know.'

74

'Sorry?'

'Leaving the country. Bit extreme teenage rebellion, don't you think? Especially as you're too old for that, now.'

Right. Not very polite hostess. 'I had an excellent job opportunity and they understood. They support me.'

Daisy cut across her. 'What job? Playing at detective? You should be at home looking after your poor father.'

'You may not speak about Henry Crow,' Lydia said flatly.

Some vestige of her father's power must still have been floating around the family as Daisy shut her mouth instantly.

'I'll be in touch,' Lydia said, as the door swung closed.

STANDING OUTSIDE THE HOUSE, Lydia took a deep breath and let it out slowly. The woman is upset, she told herself. *Don't take it personally.* More to the point, it appeared that Charlie hadn't been blowing smoke. Maddie really had walked out of her charmed life.

The house next door to Aunt Daisy's had a bay window facing the street. There were wooden slated blinds pulled low, and Lydia caught sight of movement. Slats which had been held open for a better view, falling back into place. *Nosy neighbour.*

Lydia walked up the path and knocked on the door. There was a CCTV camera bolted above the corner of the porch, directed downward and another one on the side of the house facing out. Dummy cameras were popular with those short on cash, but this was expensive real estate and from this distance, at least, they looked like the real deal. *God bless the paranoid rich.*

The door opened on a chain and a firm voice came from within. 'Hello?'

Lydia plastered on her friendliest, most unthreatening smile. 'Hi, I'm Daisy's niece. From next door?'

75

'Sorry?'

'I'm from next door,' Lydia said. 'May I speak to you for a moment?'

The chain unlatched and the door swung open fully. The woman had to be in her eighties. She had wispy grey hair held back with a wide Alice band and a leisure suit which looked like it was made of velvet.

'I'm really sorry to bother you, but Daisy said you wouldn't mind. She said you've always been a treasure in the street.' Lydia had no idea whether Daisy and John were friendly with their neighbours, but the first rule of getting people to do things for you was to give them a reason to live up to your good view of them.

'Daisy next door?' The woman's forehead creased. 'Are you Madeleine?'

'No, I'm Daisy's niece. Lydia.'

'Of course,' the woman shook her head lightly. 'Silly me. You look just like her.' Her eyes travelled the length of Lydia's body, taking in her leather jacket, jeans and combat boots. 'Well. Madeleine has a rather different style palette.'

'I was hoping I could speak to you about Madeleine, actually.' Lydia glanced around as if worried she would be overheard. 'Something terrible has happened and my family are at their wits' end.'

The promise of juicy gossip, the reminder of the Crow Family, or old-fashioned helpfulness. Whatever the reason, the woman stepped back. 'You'd better come inside.'

Lydia stepped into a wide entrance hall with dark green walls and white architrave. An umbrella stand in the shape of an elephant's foot which Lydia fervently hoped wasn't real and a coat rack with one beige mackintosh and a Barbour wax jacket, both female and small. The neighbour appeared to live alone.

'I'm Mrs Bedi. You can call me Elspeth.'

'Thank you, Elspeth,' Lydia said, crouching down to unlace her boots.

'Oh, leave those, dear. The dogs bring in all sorts so I don't worry.'

Dogs. That explained the smell.

Elspeth led the way into a living room stuffed with furniture. A pale green upright sofa and matching chairs were the only modern additions amongst Moroccan leather pouffes, brightly-embroidered Indian floor cushions, and intricately engraved brass candlesticks and spice boxes. The slatted window blinds were complemented by the ceiling fan which Lydia wouldn't have been surprised to learn had been shipped back from India when the colonial rule ended.

'You have a beautiful home,' Lydia said, still on her best behaviour.

Elspeth inclined her head slightly in acknowledgement of the compliment. 'I'm very sorry to hear of Daisy and John's trouble but I'm not sure how I can help.'

'Maddie, my cousin, has been missing for several days. They are frantic with worry.'

'That's a shame,' Elspeth said. 'How old is the girl?'

'Nineteen,' Lydia said.

Elspeth clicked her tongue against her teeth. 'Difficult age. Especially these days.' She lowered herself carefully into an armchair. 'I'm surprised I haven't been visited by the police. Door-to-door enquiries would be standard, one would have thought.'

It took Lydia a second to catch up. Elspeth might not have been about to run a marathon but she was clearly in full command of her faculties. 'They haven't been to the police. Which is why I'm trying to find her myself.'

'You?' Elspeth frowned. 'You ought to engage the authorities. It's what one pays taxes for, after all.'

Lydia took a risk. She leaned forward and make her expression pained and earnest. 'I couldn't agree more, but

77

they won't have it. Well,' she paused, biting her lip as if unsure whether to reveal a secret. 'I shouldn't really say. It's private business but my Uncle John won't hear of it. Aunt Daisy is all set to go behind his back and call the police anyway, but after the way things have been...'

Lydia let herself trail off.

Elspeth's expression was hard to read, but the tone of her voice was significantly warmer when she spoke. 'Husbands always think they know best.'

'I don't want to make things worse, but I do want to help. And I'm sure I can find Maddie without any more fuss. I just need a bit of help. Did you know Madeleine, at all?'

'I'm afraid not,' Elspeth said. 'The dogs got into their garden one time, and Madeleine helped me to round them up. She was very polite. But we're not what you would call close neighbours in this street. The sense of community isn't what it used to be. So many newcomers.'

Lydia nodded. 'Does it feel less safe here these days?'

'I'm sorry?' Elspeth looked offended. 'This is still a very good area. Very good.'

'Forgive me,' Lydia said. 'I couldn't help but notice your cameras.'

'Oh, yes. Those.' Elspeth picked at an invisible piece of fluff on her trousers. 'After Akal passed I wanted some extra security.'

'Very sensible,' Lydia said. 'Do you record all the time?' *Please say yes.*

Elspeth nodded. 'I believe so. The chap from the company set them up, of course. I don't often view the videos. Only if I'm concerned by something.'

'Madeleine hasn't been home for a week. Is there any chance you were recording on the day she left?'

'An excellent chance.' Elspeth said, rising to her feet. 'I will fetch my computer.'

She returned after a short time with a rose-gold laptop

and glasses case, both of which matched her sequinned trainers. After a period of waiting for Elspeth to log into her system and find the correct folder, during which Lydia forced herself to sit patiently by digging the nails of one hand into her palm and counting backwards from one hundred, Elspeth peered over the top of her reading glasses and said: 'Tuesday the fifteenth?'

'I'd love to see as much as you have,' Lydia said. 'I don't know what I'm looking for exactly or when it might have happened. Any insight into life at the house would be welcome. Unusual visitors, that kind of thing.'

Elspeth nodded. After another moment, she let out an irritated sigh. 'Did you want to take a look?'

She passed the laptop across and Lydia saw a software interface for 'Safe As Houses Security'. Swiftly, Lydia plugged a data stick that she readied into the USB port. 'I'll just take the relevant files so that I can leave you in peace.'

'You don't have to rush off,' Elspeth said. 'I was going to make us tea.'

'Tea would be lovely,' Lydia said. 'As long as it's no bother.'

While Elspeth was in the kitchen, Lydia located the video files set to copying them to the data stick. There were ten days of videos and a quick look in the 'settings' section of the app showed that Elspeth, or whoever installed the system, had it set to store two weeks at a time, with the oldest files wiped in blocks at the end of each period. The files were huge and the progress bar was moving slowly, so Lydia concentrated on friendly conversation and plenty of compliments to Elspeth over the rank-tasting herbal tea and the fine bone china it was served in. By the time she had run out of ways to say 'you have a lovely home' and 'yes, nettle and ginseng tea is surprisingly enjoyable', the data had, mercifully, copied across.

After giving effusive thanks and her phone number with

the instruction to 'call anytime', Lydia made her escape. Outside, the air had cooled and drops of rain spat from the darkening sky. Lydia zipped up her jacket and stuffed her hands into the pockets. The smooth curves of the USB stick promised its secrets. Lydia could only hope at least some of them would involve Maddie's mysterious disappearance.

CHAPTER SEVEN

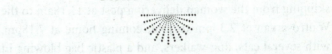

Back at the flat, alone at her makeshift workspace in the living room, Lydia allowed herself to admit that she was shaken. She didn't admit it out loud, of course, but she poured a splash of bourbon into her coffee before settling down to view the camera footage. As the caffeine and alcohol took away the after-taste of the nettle tea, Lydia realised that she had been expecting to find Madeleine holed up in her bedroom, hiding from her friends after some Millennial drama bullshit. Or to discover that Daisy and John were colluding in a ridiculous fiction with Charlie just to keep Lydia close by for whatever Machiavellian plot Charlie had concocted. Faced with the fact that Madeleine really was missing, Lydia felt sick.

Like most recorded CCTV, the footage had been stored in a low-resolution format to save space, so Lydia was treated to hour after hour of grainy imagery. Mostly of a quiet street, the edge of Elspeth's house and a small slice of her neighbouring property's front garden. Luckily enough, the cameras were set to record with a motion-detector which cut down on the footage times considerably. Luckier still, the viewing area included Madeleine's gate. On the morning on which Daisy had told Lydia Madeleine had left early, dressed for work, Lydia saw her cousin doing just that. She turned right, in the direction of the nearest tube station. The angle and video quality made it hard to glean anything significant about Maddie's demeanour. So, that was that. She watched the rest of the day on triple-speed, skipping from the woman delivering post at 11.18am to the Waitrose van at 2.34pm to John coming home at 7.18pm, with several cats, dog-walkers, and a plastic bag blowing in the wind, in between. Madeleine didn't return. Lydia took a fortifying sip of her spiked coffee and prepared to skim through the intervening days to the present date.

At half past eight in the evening on the eighteenth, there was a peculiar stretch of recording. The motion-sensor had been activated but there was no viewable footage. The screen was filled with grey snow for just under two minutes. An hour later, the same thing.

The eighteenth. That meant that it took three days after Maddie was last seen by her family for Charlie to visit the house. At least she assumed that was the cause of the interference. The small amount of power which still ran through the main bloodline of the Crow Family had a variety of effects, most of them extremely minor. The only other Crow Family member who was powerful enough to affect a camera in that way was her own father. She remembered her dad telling her about the time he and Charlie had sneaked into a theme park after hours and hadn't had to worry about the security cameras because all the guards would see would be grey snow. And, when Lydia had been older, she had asked Henry why he didn't show up in the digital pictures she attempted to take with her phone. He had given her an explanation which had been heavy on physics and Lydia, who had been expecting something magical and exciting, had tuned out as he discussed wave lengths and electrons. Looking at the snow on her screen, now, Lydia made a mental note to ask the question again and to have another go at understanding the answer.

She picked up her phone and texted Charlie, just to confirm her suspicions. Twenty-four minutes of scrolling through footage later, and she got her reply. 'Saw D&J Friday PM. Why?'

Putting the phone down, Lydia made a fresh coffee, spiked it with another generous slosh of bourbon and soldiered on.

Three hours later and Lydia was none the wiser. The email from Maddie's computer suggested that something had happened at work. She would be 'missed at the office' but the CCTV footage showed her leaving the house on the morning of her disappearance, dressed in work-appropriate clothes. Job hunting? Or perhaps Verity had just been referring to a short absence. An illness or suspension. Perhaps, like Lydia, Maddie had been encouraged to take a temporary break.

THE FOYER of the Camberwell nick was nicer than Lydia remembered. It was true, the last time she had been inside she had been distracted by the impending doom that was her father arriving to collect her after a teenage misadventure, but she still thought the place had been given a face lift. There was a giant potted plant in one corner and a low table with magazines, like a doctor's waiting room.

She asked for Fleet at the front desk and sat down on one of the chairs to wait. She had a paperback book and all the time in the world. Charlie had enlisted a cleaning crew to go through the cafe and the noise travelled upstairs, so Lydia was quite happy for the excuse to stay out of the flat. She had considered phoning him to complain and to point out that he had lied to her, again, but something stopped her. The feeling that contact from her was exactly what he wanted. That she was being tested in some way that she didn't yet understand.

Lydia flipped to her bookmarked page, desperate to escape the looping, paranoid thoughts, but she heard footsteps on the hard tiles. Lydia expected a subordinate but it was the man himself. DCI Fleet held out his hand and Lydia took it before standing. Upright, with as straight a spine as she could manage, she was still dwarfed next to him. It made her feel both unnerved and worryingly aroused. Not the time, she told her libido, firmly. When he greeted her, his voice didn't help matters. It was deep and rounded with just the right hint of south London in his accent to make her stomach go wobbly.

'I've remembered something.' Lydia kept her voice clipped and professional in the hopes it would douse the flames which Fleet irritatingly ignited. At least the misery of the institutional setting would help to keep her mind on business. Perhaps he had a nice windowless office with the smell of copier fluid and feet. That would help.

'Let's get out of here,' Fleet said, smiling at her in an unnervingly unprofessional manner. 'If you don't mind a walk?'

'Not at all.' Lydia stopped herself from returning his charismatic smile by scowling instead. It was a good scowl. One which usually made people visibly recoil, but Fleet opened the door for her and turned up the volume on his own smile as if she had fallen at his feet. Annoying. He had the kind of confidence that was almost as powerful as magic.

Outside, they picked their way through hipster boys and girls, and the occasional family. It was mid-morning and the office crowds were chained to their desks and the night-time lot were fast asleep. Fleet didn't speak until they were off the main drag and cutting down one of the old streets towards Burgess Park. It used to be an area filled with warehouses and factories and now it was a huge green space with play areas and planting. Looking around, it was hard to believe that the space used to hold the Surrey canal, which had been filled in after one too many kids drowned in its dank waters.

'So,' Fleet glanced down. 'What's up?'

'Has he woken up yet?'

Fleet hesitated. Then he nodded. 'He's not saying much, though.'

'Name?'

'John Smith.'

They shared a quick smile. John Smith was like Joe Bloggs. It was basically a middle-finger at the question.

'Your turn,' Fleet said, his expression turning serious. 'Have you remembered something else?'

Lydia was glad of her sunglasses as she looked at the cop, trying to work out how much to say. 'Nobody knows that I'm staying at The Fork. I had only just arrived. I was wondering whether there has been increased activity recently. In that street. A spate of break-ins or something?'

'Crims know that The Fork belongs to the Charlie Crow. I don't see it as a random target.'

Lydia felt disloyal, but Charlie had said 'no cops' regarding Maddie's disappearance. He hadn't expressly forbidden them for Lydia. Probably because she hadn't given him the chance, but still. She needed to point Fleet into a more general 'Crow' angle in the hope that he might turn up something useful.

Lydia nodded. 'And robbery doesn't make that much sense, anyway. Why hit that building? It's not in use, so definitely no cash in the till. Industrial kitchen equipment might be valuable, but he didn't have a van, did he?'

'Not that we have found.' Fleet said.

They had reached the park and Lydia headed to her favourite spot – the old ironwork bridge which remained from the old canal. Now, of course, it spanned an innocent patch of grass and looked like an odd kind of folly. The locals called it the 'bridge to nowhere' and, as Lydia and Fleet walked up the steps, she tried not to think that it was an apt location for her chat with the law. Halfway along the bridge, Lydia stopped and pretended to admire the view while she formulated her next line. After a few seconds of thought, she decided to dispense with subtle. It had never been her style, anyway. 'Has there been any activity with the Crows? Anything that might inspire retaliation?'

Silence.

Lydia turned to look at Fleet. He had his hands stuck in his coat pockets and was wearing a perfectly blank expression. One that was probably handed out on the last day of detective school. 'I would have thought you are better placed to answer that.'

'I told you, I just came back from Scotland. I'm not a part of anything.'

'But you attracted our friendly Mr John Smith.'

'Yes,' Lydia said. 'Exactly.' She looked into his face, making sure she didn't let her eyes flicker and waited.

Eventually, Fleet said: 'We are treating this as an isolated incident at the moment. Unless you have some other information to share?'

'No,' Lydia said. 'And thank you for meeting with me. I know you are very busy.' That was from Karen. She had always said to be super-polite to the police, you never knew who you might be able to develop into a useful contact.

Fleet didn't smile. 'It's my job.'

'Right,' Lydia said.

'You didn't need to check. I am well aware of the pressure that comes with a case like yours.'

'Pressure?'

He looked away. 'You're Charlie Crow's niece, Henry Crow's daughter. I reckon I'm going to hear about that.'

Sudden panic. 'You don't need to involve my parents. They have nothing to do with this. They don't know anything.'

'I wouldn't dare bother them,' Fleet said, his voice dry as dust.

'Great,' Lydia said. 'Thanks.'

There was a short silence and, even though she knew better, Lydia couldn't stop herself from filling it.

'So, what angles are you looking at? Who might want to attack a Crow kid?'

'Kid?'

'I'm only twenty-seven,' Lydia said, mock-affronted. If she could get Fleet looking into a general Crow attack, he might throw up something on Madeleine. It came with it the danger that Fleet might stumble into something Charlie would prefer stayed hidden, but Madeleine was missing, maybe in real danger. That had to be the priority.

They resumed walking, continuing over the bridge and then doubling-back underneath it to head back toward the park exit.

'So, have you remembered anything else? Any details?'

'No,' Lydia said. She didn't want to add anything that might send him in a particular direction. Not yet, anyway. Maybe when she made headway with her own investigation she would feed him details, use the resources at his disposal. She was painfully aware of how adrift she was in London. In Aberdeen she had made friends with a couple of law types and she had the weight of the agency behind her. Here she had nothing. Or, more accurately, she had the full weight of the Crow Family which was a complicated advantage.

Fleet interrupted her chain of thought by stopping suddenly.

'What?'

Fleet's head was tilted, his eyes appraising her. 'Mr Smith

didn't succeed. He was going to push you off the roof, but you managed to get the advantage and he went over instead.'

'Yes,' Lydia said, tensing for more questions on that awkward detail.

'He is quite a bit taller and larger than you. You must be stronger than you look.'

Lydia forced herself to look directly into Fleet's eyes. 'He must have had a weak heart or I had an adrenaline surge or something.'

'Uh-huh.' Fleet said. 'That's the story.' He resumed his steady pace and Lydia followed, wondering how much the detective knew, how much he suspected.

A group of nursery kids, roped together like husky dogs was ploughing down the path ahead and Lydia was forced to step into the road to avoid them. Once the group with the grim-faced chaperones had passed, she rejoined Fleet. 'So, will you look into it? As an angle? I'm not suggesting it ought to be high priority-'

'It's my manor,' Fleet said, sounding suddenly very pissed off.

'Sorry,' Lydia said. 'I didn't mean... Just, resources must be tight...' She trailed off.

Fleet straightened his impressive shoulders and gave her a level look. 'I will get to the bottom of this matter and bring the person or persons to justice. You have my word.'

'That's good,' Lydia said.

Fleet's eyes were cold and appraising and suddenly Lydia wasn't so sure going to the cops had been her best idea.

ON HER WAY back to the cafe, Lydia went over what she knew. Madeleine Crow had been missing for over a week and a man had broken into a Crow building and attempted to kill her. However unthinkable, it seemed unlikely that the two were unconnected. By the time she got back to the bare flat she was jumpy and in need of a stiff drink. Unfortunately, it was too early. Lydia had a strict rule – no spirits before five o'clock. The temptation to take the edge off the world was ever-present and she was wary of giving into it. She would work the case, instead.

Some of the St A's crew had gone on to university, one was planning her wedding which was, apparently, a full-time job, but Madeleine was taking a gap year and doing a part-time internship in a PR firm in Soho. Madeleine's best friend was called Sasha and they, apparently, spent most evenings together either out or at Sasha's Kensington flat. Uncle Charlie had passed on all of this information, but it had come to him via Daisy and Lydia knew that what a nineteen year old told her parents and the way in which she was truly spending her time were not necessarily the same thing.

She started with Sasha, getting the tube across town for the personal touch. The flat was on the middle floor of a white stuccoed regency beauty. Camberwell had some very fine buildings, but nothing like this. The place had a row of coach-houses behind for crying out loud.

A male voice answered when Lydia pressed the buzzer. 'I'm here to see Sasha. It's about Madeleine Crow.'

No answer, but a buzz and a click as the front door was unlocked. Lydia took the stairs two at a time, mindful of the fact that she hadn't been to the gym in five days and needed to keep her fitness up. She had no intention of becoming like Rab, the oldest investigator on the books at Karen's agency, who could barely fit his belly behind the steering wheel of his ancient BMW and could only do strictly vehicular or static surveillance.

A man opened the flat door, his expression hard to read beneath his carefully-sculpted facial hair. He had a giant Tin Tin style quiff which Lydia couldn't help admiring and he looked to be in his mid-twenties, at least. 'Sash is through here.' He led the way to a gigantic open plan space with stripped wooden flooring and light flooding through generously-proportioned windows. The walls were white, the light fittings copper and vaguely industrial-looking, and the oriental rug had probably cost more than Lydia's car. Sasha was curled up on the white sofa, dressed head-to-toe in soft layers of dove grey cashmere and bamboo. She didn't look like any teenager Lydia had previously known. But, then, the flat was like nothing she could imagine owning under the age of twenty. Scratch that, Lydia look around again, trying not let her jaw drop; the place wasn't like anything she could imagine owning ever in her life.

'Perry,' Sasha said. 'Be a darling and make some coffee.' It wasn't a question.

Perry ambled off and Sasha regarded Lydia from behind her fringe. She had long flaxen hair lying perfectly straight around her face, so the strands which fell into her eyes must have been there deliberately. Lydia didn't think anything in this room would dare to be out of place. How old was this self-possessed, perfectly-presented human? It seemed impossible that she was nineteen like Madeleine. The rich truly were a breed apart.

She wasn't, however, a member of any of the families, and Lydia couldn't see a single spark of magic. Perhaps she was Madeleine's 'normal friend' in the way that Emma was hers.

'I'm here to talk to you about Madeleine. I'm her cousin.'

Sasha lifted her chin. 'Do you have a name?'

'Lydia Crow,' Lydia said.

Sasha straightened a little. 'Sit down, if you want.'

Lydia perched on the edge of a battered leather armchair. It looked as if it had been rescued from the library of a stately home but was probably brand new from Anthropologie.

'When did you last hear from Madeleine?'

90

'I've already been through all of this with Maddie's uncle.'

'I know,' Lydia said, 'but everyone is really worried. They've asked me to help.'

'As I told Mr Crow, I haven't seen Madeleine since the CSV event.'

'And when was that?' Lydia got out her phone to make notes and looked at it to hide her irritation. These were not state secrets.

Nothing. Lydia looked up. Sasha was gazing out of the window.

'Sasha?'

Slowly, Sasha turned her head back to face Lydia. 'Has nobody seen her?'

'No,' Lydia said. 'We're all really worried.'

Sasha pressed her lips together. 'I didn't think it would matter.'

Perry walked back in carrying a tray with two espresso cups. He put it down on the coffee table and made to sit on the sofa.

'No.' Sasha said and Perry straightened up immediately. He put one hand on his hip and frowned at her. 'What has Perry done, now?'

Good grief. Talked about himself in the third person, for starters. Lydia had been feeling sorry for the hirsute man-child, but now she wasn't so sure. They were both awful.

Sasha waited until Perry had left the room before indicating that Lydia should take a cup from the tray.

'No, thank you.' Lydia lowered her voice. 'When did you last see Madeleine?'

'We did go to the CSV event, but I told Mr Crow it was on the eleventh.'

Five days before she went missing. 'When was it, really?'

'Two months ago.'

She had the grace to look momentarily contrite. 'I didn't

91

think it would matter. When Mr Crow asked, I thought he was going to find her later that day. She would, I don't know, call or something. Or just turn up.'

'It's okay,' Lydia said.

'She's really not the type to run away. That would take too much effort.'

Lydia put a little bit of steel into her voice. 'What matters is that you're telling the truth now.'

Sasha's eyes widened. 'Just a simple misunderstanding-'

'Why did it happen? The misunderstanding?'

'I didn't want to say that I hadn't seen Maddie. I didn't know what she -' Sasha broke off.

'You didn't know what she had told her parents and didn't want to get her into trouble.'

Sasha nodded.

'Is it normal for the two of you to go so long without contact?'

'Oh, we've been in contact. I just haven't *seen* seen her. You know?'

'You've spoken?'

'We've both been on Insta. She's been liking my stuff.'

'But you haven't seen her or spoken to her. Not directly.'

'She's fine, you really don't have to worry.'

'I'm sure she is,' Lydia said. 'But I still have to find her. And you didn't answer my question.'

'Which one?'

'Is it normal for you to go two months without seeing your best mate?'

Sasha shook her head. 'Things have been a bit weird. We kind of fell out. She was so drunk at the CSV event, it was embarrassing.'

Lydia pulled a sympathetic face. 'It was good of you not to tell Uncle Charlie, that. I know you've been protecting her, being a good friend.'

'I have,' Sasha straightened up for the first time. She

leaned forward and picked up her espresso, taking a delicate sip. 'We're too old for that, now. It was a work thing and she was slurring and falling over. I was mortified.'

'Your work thing or hers?'

'Mine. You know she's interning with Minty?'

Lydia smiled and nodded, channelling friendly compatriot with all her being. She even reached for the disgustingly strong coffee and pretended to drink.

'Well, I'm there, too. Daddy got me in no problem because of my grades and on account of my previous experience, but he really had to call in a big favour for them to take Maddie as well. There isn't quite as much for her to do, but it's a golden opportunity for her. Not the sort of thing she's likely to get ever again.'

Lydia felt a spurt of sympathy for Madeleine. If this creature was her best friend, no wonder she had wanted to run away from her life. 'So you argued? Was this on the night or after?'

Sasha put her cup down carefully. 'Both. She wasn't in a state to understand the gravity of the situation on the night.'

The phrase had a false ring. Maybe something which had been said to Sasha in the past and now she was enjoying the chance to use it about somebody else. 'You called her the next day?'

Sasha pulled a face, either trying to remember, or working out how to phrase things to put herself in the best light. 'I didn't think she would be up to it the day after and I was busy. I do have a life, after all. It must have been on the weekend, a couple of days after. We were supposed to be doing lunch but I sent her a text.'

'To cancel?'

Sasha nodded. 'I said I was still upset with her and didn't feel emotionally ready for IRL contact.'

'She replied?'

'No.'

'Can I see the text?'

Sasha reared back like a pony. 'No! I'm not showing you my phone.'

'Fair enough,' Lydia said. 'If I give you my number, could you forward it to me?'

'It's private correspondence.'

Lydia was suddenly out of patience. 'If you forward me the text and give me your solemn and binding word that you will notify me immediately if Madeleine gets in touch or you remember anything else whatsoever about the time before or after she disappeared, I will conveniently forget to inform Charlie Crow that you lied to him.'

There was a short silence while Sasha contemplated this generous offer. Sasha might not have magical lineage but she wasn't stupid. She kept her eyes on Lydia and raised her voice to a piercing level. 'Perry!'

The man-child appeared. Was he her lover, friend or butler? It was impossible to tell.

'What is it, darling?'

'Phone.'

'Right-o.'

Once Perry had fetched an iPhone – the latest model, naturally, and Sasha had swiped at it with ill-concealed fury and forwarded on her less-measured-than-she-had-indicated text, Lydia took her leave of the unhappy tableau.

'See her out,' Sasha said and closed her eyes.

At the door, Perry seemed about to apologise for Sasha but then he just offered an oddly lack lustre, 'Take care, now.'

SPOILED PR-WANNABES, aside, Lydia wasn't having the best day. The cleaning crew had done a frighteningly good job of smartening up The Fork and her hopes that Uncle Charlie had been telling the truth about 'not really opening' had hit rock bottom. The place smelled of bleach and fresh paint.

At least the place was empty and quiet for now. Lydia looked around and tried not to be impressed by the transformation. With the layer of grime removed, the original 1930s cream and black tiles which lined the walls looked suddenly charming, and the new red flooring brought the whole room to life. The windows were sparkling and the yellowed white nets had been replaced with a cheerful red gingham check. The glass-fronted counter had also been scrubbed clean. The shabby tables and chairs were the same but they now looked retro rather than rank.

The swing door to the kitchen opened and Lydia swore. 'You scared me.'

Angel didn't apologise or, in fact, acknowledge Lydia's presence. She put down the pile of crockery she was carrying onto the large wooden buffet and disappeared back into the kitchen.

Lydia pulled the burner phone from her pocket and called Charlie. 'What happened to 'no renovations'?'

'Lyds, sweetheart. You are a mind-reader.'

Lydia closed her eyes.

'I was just thinking about you. Any news on Maddie?'

'That's not why I'm calling. The Fork. It's been cleaned and decorated and Angel is cooking for the masses. You told me –'

Charlie interrupted. 'How does it look?'

'Brilliant,' Lydia said, truthfully. 'That's not the point, though.' Another thought crossed her mind. 'And since when did the Pearls have shops in Camberwell?'

There was a beat of silence. 'I told you things had changed.'

CHAPTER EIGHT

Lydia slipped her phone back into her pocket and ran up the stairs to her flat, trying to expend her nervous energy through the burn in her muscles. She was annoyed with herself for being annoyed with Charlie. She knew what he was like, so why was she surprised? It made her feel stupid, though, which in turn made her feel angry. And a bit frightened.

The ghost was hovering outside the door to her bedroom. Not in the sense of levitating, but in the sense of looking uncharacteristically nervous. 'There you are,' he said.

'Here I am,' Lydia agreed, edging past her non-corporeal house mate. She wasn't in the mood for another bickering match.

'Why are you here?'

Lydia took off her jacket and threw it over the chair she had brought up from downstairs for just that purpose, and began going through her clothes for something suitable to wear that evening. If she ignored the ghost, perhaps he would move out.

She felt cool air on her back, the hairs on her neck lifting.

'Don't you have a home of your own?'

'I told you,' Lydia said, glancing at the ghost. 'I'm just crashing for a few days.'

He shifted and the movement made Lydia feel sick. She turned back to the mess of clothes on the bed. She really needed to get some drawers or something. Maybe a hanging rail. The thought brought her up short. *She didn't need furniture because she wasn't staying.*

'I need to ask you something,' the ghost said, his voice uncomfortably close and creepily breathy.

Lydia turned and looked him in the eye. 'Are you going to tell me your name?'

He glanced away and didn't answer.

'Then, no. You are rude and I'm not going to answer your questions.'

The ghost looked miserable and Lydia felt a stab of guilt for being mean to the dead guy. He was already having a pretty bad day.

There. Her favourite 'smart' T-shirt. Black, like all her tops, but made from a silky material which draped nicely from the slash-neck. She sniffed it. Clean enough. 'I'm going to get changed, so if you don't mind...' She looked over her shoulder, but the ghost had already gone.

EMMA WALKED UP to meet Lydia in a state of high excitement. 'Look at the time! Look!'

It was almost ten and there was a queue outside Club Foxy which they joined. 'Thank you for coming,' Lydia said.

'Are you kidding? I'm usually comatose in front of my Downton boxset at this time of night. It's tragic.' Emma gestured at the queue of clubbers. 'This is the most excitement I've had in months. Years, probably.'

'When did you and Tom last go out together?'

Emma pulled a face. 'On our own? God, I don't know. Ages. New Year's Eve, maybe?'

The gulf between their lives yawned between them. 'You aren't missing much,' Lydia said quickly. 'Trust me.'

'I don't want to be on the market,' Emma said, as the queue shuffled forward. 'It would just be nice to be part of couple sometimes, not just a cog in the parenting machine.'

A girl with black hair and a septum piercing turned around from her own friends and fixed Emma with a drunken smile. 'You have babies? That is so cute. I love babies.'

Emma gave her a polite smile.

'In you go, ladies.' They had reached the front and the bouncer waved them in. They paid and the rabbity guy in the booth stamped Emma's hand with a stylised fox head which made Lydia's stomach turn. 'I'm fine,' she said, not offering her hand.

'You gotta get a stamp.'

'I'll take my chances,' Lydia said and wrenched open the black door.

Inside, they were hit by a wall of sound and heat. The bass was thumping and bodies gyrated on a tiny dance floor, which was lined on one side by a massive glittering bar and booth-style seating around the others. Stairs to their right led to the mezzanine level and Lydia could see men leaning on the railings above. The crowd was an odd mix and not the kind of place she would have put her rich young cousin. Reading the room she was relieved not to get a strong Fox vibe. Perhaps the name was a coincidence. It wasn't as if they had a trademark on it, after all.

Lydia was still trying to convince herself that she wasn't in the Foxes' den when she spotted one. Paul Fox. He was leaning against the bar, near to where Emma was being served. Lydia had grabbed a spare booth and was guarding their seating. She watched as he lazily scanned the room. He had the same lithe body and animal magnetism that she remembered from their brief, ill-advised fling. It had been stupid. She had been stupid. Her aunt Daisy was wrong – she hadn't been rebelling by going to Scotland, she had been trying to halt a far worse course of action. Paul Fox had been a very bad idea and she had known that the only way to break the spell he had over her was to put miles between them.

She tested herself, now, watching him. Was there any attraction there? Did she feel the old pull? The slim face was just as handsome, the curve of his aristocratic eyebrows and thin lips just as pleasingly arranged. Put him in a frilled shirt and breeches and he would fit right into a period drama. But she felt okay. No desire to walk up and climb him. With that thought, the image of DCI Fleet jumped into her mind. Now that was a man she could climb. He looked like he could hold her up with one arm which would leave the other hand free to...

Emma put two bottles of beer down on the table and Lydia blinked.

'Twelve quid. Two beers, twelve quid. I was going to get us cocktails, to celebrate, but I would have needed a second mortgage.'

Emma's voice was barely audible above the music, even though Lydia could tell she was shouting. Lydia grabbed her beer and took a grateful swallow. Less lust, more investigating.

'Cheers!' Emma clinked her bottle against Lydia's.

She scooched in close on the smooth seating so that she could speak directly into Emma's ear. 'My ex is at the bar. Don't look.'

Too late, of course. Emma had done the thing that every single person in the entire history of human interaction has ever done when told not to look. She looked.

'Yum.'

'I know,' Lydia said with feeling.

'Was that the one you were seeing before –'

Lydia nodded.

'Christ,' Emma said and took a long pull on her beer. 'You were a fucking mess.'

Lydia drank to avoid agreeing out loud. Emma was right and Lydia was mentally kicking herself for not preparing for this possibility. She realised that she had been kidding herself, thinking that she could come back to London and work a job for Charlie without encountering her old life. This so-called holiday back with in the bosom of her family had turned into so much more, and Lydia couldn't help feeling that she had solved one problem by creating a much bigger one. Like trying to douse a fire with a glass of whisky.

She risked another glance, but Paul Fox had gone. A quick look around revealed that he was nowhere to be seen. Lydia put her head back and looked at the lights reflected by the gold-tinted mirrors which lined the walls. Thousands of golden-hued party-goers were drinking and dancing and shouting at one another. Lydia felt suddenly very tired. What was she doing here? What did she think she was going to find in London?

'So,' Emma put down her beer and leaned in close enough that Lydia could feel her breath on her cheek and smell Emma's perfume. 'What are we looking for?'

For a moment Lydia thought that Emma had added 'mind-reader' to her list of incredible qualities and then she realised that she meant in the practical sense. 'I don't know. Madeleine came here with a group of friends before she disappeared.'

'Right before?'

Lydia nodded. Madeleine's mother had heard her come home that night, at half past one, but she didn't see her daughter. The next day, she and John had both gone to work, assuming that Madeleine had left earlier for work or was sleeping off a hangover.

'Was this what you expected?'

'I don't know. It's not anything, really. Not A-list glam or rebellious grunge. I'm surprised Madeleine's crowd bothered with it.' Lydia looked around. It was a perfectly normal, perfectly decent nightclub. Although it contained at least one Fox. And, if it was linked to that Family, won the unsubtle name of the year award.

'Did you want to dance or shall we get to work?'

'Work first,' Emma said. 'And I'm going to need another drink.'

Lydia tried one of the security men, first. He was standing by a door which led to the fire escape, stopping people from using it as a smoking spot and setting off the alarm. Lydia listened as he turned away three people and a couple who were half undressed and looking for a dark corner.

She held up a photograph of Madeleine. A studio portrait courtesy of Daisy in which she looked wholesome, perfect, and nowhere near old enough to be drinking. The bouncer barely glanced at it before he was shaking his head. 'We get a lot of girls in here.'

'She's nineteen,' Lydia tried to keep her voice friendly while simultaneously having to yell over the pumping music. 'The club hasn't done anything wrong. I'm just trying to find her.'

'Why?' The man inclined his head. 'Girlfriend?'

'Cousin,' Lydia said. She pulled out a photo she had blown up and printed from Madeleine's Insta feed. It was the one which showed mostly Madeleine, smiling and fully-made-up and wearing a small sparkly halter top. In this one she could have been anything from sixteen to well-preserved thirty.

The bouncer took a longer look this time. No longer fearful that Lydia was about to shop the club for serving a minor. He frowned, obviously concentrating and Lydia felt hope leap in her chest. Eventually, though, he shrugged. 'Dunno. Maybe seen her? Was this last summer, yeah?'

'Two weeks ago. She came in with a group of friends. All female, I think.'

Lydia used her phone to show the man the rest of the Instagram pictures, clearly taken in the club.

'What night was this?'

Lydia told him, pointing at the date on the screen for additional clarity.

'You should speak to Guy. He was working the bar that night and I bet he'll remember. They were drinking Mojitos and they are a fucking pain in the arse to make.'

THE MAIN BAR where Guy was serving was mobbed and Lydia didn't fancy conducting an interview by shouting across it. 'Do you want to dance or sit down for a while?' She yelled the question into Emma's ear and was glad when Emma yelled back 'Sit!'

It was quieter in the chill room and conversation was marginally easier. Emma sunk onto the squashy leatherette seating and immediately slipped off her heels. 'These things are fucking torture. How the hell did I used to wear them?'

Lydia put her Dr Marten's onto the low table in front of the sofa and said 'no idea'.

Once Emma had rubbed the soles of her feet and downed half of her beer she leaned close to ask. 'Okay, boss. What's next?'

Lydia didn't want to admit that she wasn't sure, but it was Emma so she did. Then, as if she had opened a tap, the words spilled out. 'I'm not sure I'm up to this. Karen had me on honeytrap duty mostly.'

Emma wrinkled her nose. 'What's that?'

'You know, you chat up some guy and see if he resists.'

'Why?'

'To see if he's faithful.'

'Bloody hell,' Emma leaned back.

'I know. Grim.' Karen started her own firm because she was sick of always being given honeytrap jobs by the male-run agency she worked for. Then, of course, she discovered that it was really lucrative. Plus, those kinds of jobs, along with basic husband or wifely surveillance were the perfect jobs for a newbie as they didn't, in general, involve criminals. In theory, it was easier to execute without being discovered, even when you made stupid mistakes like tailing too closely, and safer for the junior investigator.

'Except when the couple gets back together and start threatening violence,' Emma said.

'Exactly.' Lydia had finished her beer sometime ago and wanted another. But not in this place.

'Do you really think the business up north has followed you to London?'

'No,' Lydia said. 'But what else could it be?'

'I don't want to speak ill of your family, but...'

'No,' Lydia shook her head. 'That's the thing. It can't be Family business. The Families don't touch each other.'

'How come?'

'There's a truce.' Lydia wondered how much Emma wanted to know. When they had been at school together, Emma had never questioned her about her family and it was one of the many reasons she had bonded so closely. Emma had been one of the few people who seemed to genuinely like her for who she was, rather than the tarnished glamour of her family name.

'What about someone closer?'

'A Crow?' Lydia's first instinct was to snort derisively. Charlie had stopped all in-fighting when he took over but, as he was keen to point out, she'd been away a while. And shielded from the worst of it by her mum and dad. Little Lydia, out in the sticks and brought up as a normal. How much did she know about the Crow Family, really?

Lydia had been watching the bar from their vantage point in the corner and when Guy moved away, high-fiving a perky-looking blonde girl who appeared to be taking over from him, she got up and towed Emma over to intercept. Guy's face lit up when he caught sight of Emma blocking his way, his eyes travelling down the length of her body in a practised assessment that made Lydia want to smack him. 'Have you got a minute?' Emma said, smiling.

'Sure,' Guy upped 'looking' to 'leering'.

'Great!' Emma stepped to the side and Lydia held out the picture of Madeleine and her friends. 'You remember this girl?'

'Which one?' Guy barely glanced at the photo.

'Dark one in the middle. The one who has gone missing.'

Guy stepped back. 'I don't know anything about that.'

Lydia wished, not for the first time, that she had a bit of her dad's gleam. A little shine would zone Guy right out, make him more likely to chat. Instead, she had to rely on reputation. She produced a gold coin and watched Guy's eyes widen as he recognised it.

'Do you remember her?' Emma tapped Madeleine's face. 'Simple question.'

Guy glanced down at the picture, his eyes blank and panicked. 'Is she in trouble?'

'She's one of us,' Lydia said. 'And I want to know if you remember seeing her here. Come on, Guy. Answer us and we'll leave you alone.' She flipped the coin high into the air. Guy watched it spin, the rotation slower than it should have been, the way it moved almost lazy. Bolts of bright light seemed to come from the coin, where the lights of the club caught its bright surface. His gaze followed the coin, landing

105

on Lydia's hand when she caught it. She closed her fingers around the coin, making it disappear. When Guy looked at her, his eyes were pleading, frightened. It was a good thing he didn't know she was a damp squib, but Lydia felt worryingly comfortable with the effect her family name was having on a complete stranger. She felt powerful and guilty all at the same time and Emma's ill-concealed surprise, wasn't helping.

'Still waiting,' Lydia said.

'Last Friday, right?' He licked his lips.

'Yep,' Lydia said.

'She was here,' Guy said. 'She didn't say she was a Crow.' He held his hands up. 'I had no idea.'

'Anything happen? Any fights or hassle?'

He shook his head.

'She was with a group of friends, any of them get into any trouble?'

He shook his head again and Lydia could see he was still trying to move away. She thought her coin trick hadn't been enough and was about to offer him money, but before she could make a decision, he was talking. 'She came in with that crowd. They had a round of cocktails. But then she wasn't with them.'

'She left?'

'She was loved up with some guy and they left together. She was only here for an hour tops.'

'You know who she left with?'

'I can't say.' Guy looked down.

'Why?' Emma had one hand on a hip and had hardened her expression. 'You don't know him? You can describe him for us.'

Guy swallowed, his eyes darting around as if hoping for rescue. He was scared. And at once, Lydia knew. 'Who is your boss, here?'

Guy shook his head. 'Please don't ask me that.'

'She left with Tristan Fox?' Lydia guessed.

He shook his head, violently this time. Like he was trying to shake something loose. 'No, no, no. I can't say.'

'You're not saying,' Lydia said. 'I'm guessing. Not your fault if I guess, is it?' She swallowed. 'Paul Fox?'

Guy went still and stared at the floor. He looked like he wanted to cry.

'Got it,' Lydia said. She felt sick.

After Guy scurried off, Lydia and Emma headed for the exit.

Outside the club, Lydia leaned against the cool brick wall and took several gulps of air. It smelled of exhaust-fumes and cooking oil from the kebab place on the corner, but her fingers stopped tingling. People were still queuing outside Club Foxy and Emma was checking her watch, a curtain of hair hiding her face. When she spoke, her voice sounded funny. Strained. 'Shall we call it a night?'

'Okay,' Lydia said, willing Emma to look at her. 'Let's find a cab.'

They walked a little way down the street, towards the main thoroughfare and, sure enough, a couple of taxis were waiting. A fair number of people were on the pavements, places to go, drinks to imbibe, partners to find. Lydia was trying to process what she had learned and failing. Unhelpful thoughts like 'she's a bit young for him' with the follow-up, she's the same age you were when you fell for Paul Fox, swirled around her head.

A man staggered in front of her but kept his footing. 'All right, beautiful,' he slurred as he passed. 'Nice tits.'

Emma was watching the drunk winding his way along the pavement, not looking at Lydia. After a moment she spoke. 'How did you do that?'

'What?'

'Make the bartender talk. He didn't want to tell us anything.' Emma bit her lip. 'Was that magic?'

107

Lydia forced a laugh. 'I wish. Just the Crow rep at work.'

Emma nodded, but she still didn't look at Lydia. 'I've always known about your family. The rumours. I mean everyone knows the stories.'

'It's all right,' Lydia said. She knew what Emma meant; everybody knew the stories but nobody really believed them. Not really.

'And I know you do those coin tricks,' Emma's eyes were wide, 'I just never –'

'I didn't do anything to him, I swear,' Lydia said. 'I couldn't even if I wanted to.'

Emma nodded. 'Okay.' She walked to the first cab and opened the door. She still hadn't looked at Lydia properly.

'Text me when you get home,' Lydia said, following behind.

Emma nodded. 'Call you tomorrow.'

Lydia put a hand on her arm, just as she was climbing into the taxi. 'Are you okay?'

'Course,' Emma said, but her gaze skittered over Lydia's hairline and then to the empty space beside her, didn't land anywhere near her face.

Lydia was about to get into the next cab when a familiar figure stepped out from behind the queue of people. He put a hand on Lydia's arm and she felt a jolt of electricity. There was a musky animal scent and the tang of midwinter air and warm earth. Fox.

For a second her heart stuttered, too, thinking it was Paul. But then she looked up and it wasn't him. Definitely a Fox, though. One of Paul's brothers, perhaps. The man's face was perfectly symmetrical with the sharp cheekbones and curved lips which had made Paul Fox so irresistible to a younger Lydia. It was cold and cruel, though, with none of the cheeky warmth Paul either had or was capable of faking extremely well.

108

The hand on her arm squeezed painfully. 'You shouldn't be here, little bird.'

Lydia planted her feet and forced herself to maintain eye contact. They were in public, taxi drivers and a whole queue of clubbers to act as witness. 'What's it to you?' She pulled her arm away and he surprised her by letting go easily.

'Fly away again. Fly away fast.' He leaned in fast, one arm around her and his lips pressed to her cheek as if he were saying a friendly goodbye. It stung and Lydia put an involuntarily hand to her face.

He smiled and Lydia felt a chill, the scent of Fox was stronger and filled her nostrils, choking her. 'You take care, now, little bird.'

Lydia watched him walk away. Hands in his pockets like he didn't have a care in the world.

'You waiting, love?'

The cab driver had wound down his window, his voice tired. No doubt he had had enough of drunk clubbers forgetting what they were doing.

Lydia got into the next cab and gave her address, annoyed with her body for shaking. The Fox Family couldn't touch her. She rubbed her arm and concentrated on the more important matter of her best friend.

Emma had looked freaked. She shouldn't have questioned Guy in front of Emma, that much was obvious with the twenty-twenty of hindsight. She had scared her best friend. *Hell hawk.* The old curse fell into her mind and Lydia threw her head back against the seat in frustration. It didn't matter that she was about as powerful as a water pistol or that she knew next-to-nothing about the Family business, she was still capable of accidentally scaring a woman who had known her since she was five. She had run all the way to Scotland and back, but it hadn't solved a thing. She was still the same old Lydia; she wasn't a Crow and she wasn't normal. A foot in both worlds and belonging to neither.

What had it been like for Madeleine? Growing up in the Family, not outside it? Had she wanted to run away, too? Had she, weirdly, chosen the same act of rebellion as Lydia had at the same age? Sleeping with a Fox. Unless it wasn't her and Madeleine repeating behaviour as much as Paul Fox... Which begged the question; what did he want? And was it the same thing he wanted from her eight years ago? Lydia closed her eyes and saw the flashing lights of the club, the gold-touched bodies moving on the dance floor.

What did the Crows have that the Foxes had always wanted?

Everything.

CHAPTER NINE

Lydia slammed back through the café and up the stairs to the flat. The adrenaline of the evening was still flowing, but she knew it would drain away at any moment. She went into the bathroom and took a short, hot shower. Getting that close to a Fox had left her feeling grubby. She concentrated on the sensation of the scalding water, and on lathering and rinsing her hair, until the buried memories were safely back underground. Wrapped in a towel, and padding to the bedroom, Lydia almost screamed at the sight of the ghost waiting in the doorway.

'Hell Hawk!' Lydia said, gripping the edge of her towel and trying not to cry. 'You have to stop jumping out at me.'

'Sorry.' He looked down, his hands dangling by his sides and mumbled something else

'What? I can't hear you?'

'I didn't jump,' he said, sounding petulant. 'And I was waiting for you. I was being polite.'

'Do you expect me to say 'thank you' for not joining me in the shower?' The words were out of Lydia's mouth before she realised what she was saying. Her stomach flipped. 'Never ever do that,' she added, glowering.

He looked gratifyingly nervous. If he were alive, his feet would probably be shifting or something, but he was completely still. It was another giveaway, Lydia thought, something unnatural in the way he carried himself. She contemplated shutting the bedroom door in his face without another word. She had enough to deal with, after all, but she couldn't quite bring herself to be that cold. 'Give me a moment to get changed,' she said, instead, slipping past the motionless spirit.

After throwing on pyjama bottoms and a soft cotton vest at high speed and hanging her damp towel on the radiator, she opened the door. 'Come in if you're coming.'

The ghost slid past and Lydia resisted the urge to reach out and touch him. She wanted to see if he was as solid as he looked. 'You said you were waiting for me. What do you want?'

'How can you see me? What are you?'

'I'm just a normal person,' Lydia said.

'But nobody else has ever seen me. I woke up in this place, but after a while of practising I could leave. All I could think about was visiting my –'he broke off. 'Visiting her. But she couldn't see me. She loved me and she was grieving and I was right there.'

Crap. Lydia looked at the emotion on his face and felt even worse. 'I'm sorry,' she said. 'I don't know what to tell you.'

'There has to be something about you. You're one of them, aren't you? One of the families?'

'You know about that?' Lydia said.

He shrugged. 'My family has lived in Camberwell a long time. You hear things.'

Lydia looked away, unable to witness his raw misery any longer. 'I'm Lydia Crow. My Uncle is Charlie Crow. He owns this place.'

'So when you said 'normal' you meant in the sense of

belonging to the most powerful of the magical families in London. It's not the usual usage of the word.'

His sarcastic tone was back so Lydia risked looking at him again. Sarcasm she could handle. 'You don't understand,' Lydia said. 'Why won't you tell me your name? I don't trust a person who is cagey with the most basic of information. It's not generally a good sign. Especially in the criminally violent.'

'I'm not violent,' the man looked genuinely incensed.

'It's not that I'm not grateful,' Lydia began, wondering how to navigate the nuance of 'thank you for hitting the bad man' but 'you tossed a guy off the roof and I don't know if you are going to go all ghost-rage and do the same to me'.

'And you're the one who could do something horrible to me. I know the rumours about the Crows.'

'Then you know better than to be talking like that.'

'I know what your family does. Which is why I'm not giving you my name. You'll use it to look me up and then you'll exorcise me or whatever. I know your uncle probably sent you here on clean-up duty.'

Lydia was silent while she turned this over. It was possible that Charlie had given her a haunted building as a test. To make her slip up and reveal a power to him, perhaps. 'Does he know about you?'

'What?' The ghost looked confused. 'I don't know.'

'You said nobody had seen you before, I was just wondering-'

'He didn't seem to see me, but maybe he was faking.'

'Possible,' Lydia said. 'He is tricky like that.'

There was a short silence as Lydia weighed up how much to reveal. This was a stranger, but he wasn't really real. He was a spirit and would probably disappear at any moment. 'Thing is,' Lydia said. 'I'm not really a Crow. I'm part of the Family by blood, but I'm 'out'.'

He looked sceptical.

'Honestly,' Lydia said. 'You've got nothing to worry about. I'm not here to get rid of you or to do anything. I'm just staying for a couple of weeks and then I'll be out of your hair. No fuss no muss.'

'But you're some kind of investigator. You're doing a job for your uncle.'

'Look,' her patience disappeared. 'I was brought up outside the Family and even if I were part of the organisation I would be a very small part. Minuscule.'

'Yeah, but the Crows... I mean, it's The Crow Family. I'm not stupid, not everyone listens to the stories, but I always have. I know stuff.'

'The Crows are Big Bads, yes. Illegal back in the day and possibly still dodgy... They are powerful, yes. But I'm not.' Lydia sat on the bed. 'As far as Charlie is concerned I have no power at all. Nothing. I'm an anomaly. A genetic mistake.'

He frowned, the expression making him look more alive than ever. 'Is that true?'

'God's honest,' Lydia said. And, sadly, it was. Mostly. Truth was, she was pretty lame. Her power went as far as sensing power in others. Lydia could tell if they had a little in their family history, like the gleam she had seen around Detective Chief Inspector Fleet, or if they were the fully-loaded real deal. If a person's power was strong enough, she could pick-up on its particulars and feel if they were silver-tongued or pearly, but mainly she got a blunt 'yes or no'. She was like the security gate at the airport, beeping when somebody was packing magic. She was an appliance. In magical terms, she was basically a toaster. Now she was depressed.

'Oh,' he crossed the threshold into the room and then stopped again. Unsure. 'You're really not here to kill me?'

Lydia thought about pointing out the obvious flaw in that statement but instead she just shook her head. 'I promise. Have you been here long?'

He hesitated, then said: 'Thirty-five years.'

'Bloody hell.' He had died in the early eighties. That explained the awful suit. 'Did it happen here?'

His eyes narrowed. 'Are you trying to work out what is keeping me here? Trying to give me closure?'

'No,' Lydia said, failing to suppress a small sigh. 'I was trying to make conversation. I can stop if you like.'

He didn't reply. After a moment, Lydia decided to ignore him back. She scooted back against her pillows and picked up her book.

'It was our wedding breakfast.'

Lydia looked up. 'At The Fork?'

'Yes,' he looked defensive. 'It was nicer, then. And it was where we had our first date so...'

'That's really lovely,' Lydia said quickly. 'Romantic.'

'It was,' he said. 'Everyone came back after the church. The owner let us have the whole place and we decorated it with balloons and stuff. We had fancy drink and Amy's mother brought a trifle. The Fork laid on a buffet but she insisted, said it wasn't a party otherwise. And we had Baby-cham and Snowballs. The real ones, not knock-offs.'

'Very nice,' Lydia said.

'I'll let you get back to your reading,' he said, suddenly stiffening up, as if realising that he had been sharing too much.

'You don't have to go.' Lydia began, but he had already turned away. 'I'm sorry,' she said to his back, knowing that it was insufficient in the circumstances.

He paused and spoke without turning. 'Jason.'

'Nice to meet you,' Lydia said. 'Sleep tight, Jason.'

LYDIA HAD RECEIVED a message from Emma simply saying 'yes' when she had texted to ask if she was safely home and then nothing. Lydia couldn't stop seeing her friend's expression, the confusion which had been replaced with poorly concealed fear. Now, Emma wasn't answering her phone. Lydia had left a message on the land line answering machine, a voicemail on Emma's mobile and sent three light-hearted texts with jaunty emojis. Nothing.

NEEDING BOTH the distraction of getting out of the flat and some food, Lydia headed to the nearest Tesco Metro, giving the Pearlie grocery shop a wide-berth. She was thoughtfully squeezing an avocado when her mobile rang. It was Fleet and his voice was as deadpan as usual. 'We need to talk.'

'Fire away,' Lydia said putting down the fruit.

'Best if we do this in person,' Fleet said. 'I'm in the area right now.'

That wasn't a good sign. Lydia stuffed down her sense of foreboding and finished her grocery shopping. She put lasagne, ready-washed salad, apples, milk, a bottle of bourbon and a gigantic bag of salt and vinegar crisps into her basket and headed to the check-out.

The supermarket was only two streets away from the cafe so Lydia was surprised to find Fleet parked outside and leaning against his car, waiting. He must have been 'right outside' not just 'in the area.'

'Another house call, DCI Fleet? I'm honoured.' Lydia was trying very hard not to notice how good he looked. He was wearing a sharply cut three-piece suit, in a dark blue-ish grey with a slate-coloured shirt and burgundy tie. Combined with his height and wide shoulders, it made him look more like a fashion spread for GQ than a copper. Lydia licked her lips and tried not to wonder just how much muscle definition one would find underneath all that excellent tailoring.

He tilted his head. The smile that suggested so much more than professional courtesy was back and Lydia wondered if it was just for her. He didn't give the impression of being a habitual flirt, but Lydia didn't trust her instincts when it came to men. 'Call me Ignatius.'

'Why? Is this another social visit?'

He held out a large hand, palm face down and moved it to indicate 'so so'. He straightened up and nodded at the cafe. 'Shall we?'

Lydia unlocked the front door and tried to lead Fleet straight upstairs. Instead of following, he stood stock-still in the middle of the cafe. 'You've been busy.'

'Not me,' Lydia said, shifting her shopping from one hand to the other to give her arm a rest. Fleet dived forward, hand outstretched. 'Sorry. Let me.'

'That's okay,' Lydia said, taking a step back and almost losing her balance.

Fleet immediately went still. 'I'm sorry. I didn't mean to frighten you.'

Lydia, for no reason she could account for, suddenly felt like crying. 'You didn't,' she managed to say after a moment.

The gleam that she'd caught on him before was back. It licked around his outline and Lydia had to concentrate hard to ignore it. She covered her embarrassment by saying 'Ignatius? What kind of a name is that?'

'Pain in the arse kind.'

The tension eased and Lydia managed a smile. 'Come on up,' she said and took the stairs. Lydia pushed open the door to the living room, hoping to find it empty. A quick look around confirmed that Jason wasn't levitating by the window or anything awkward.

'Take a seat, I'll just put this away.'

Lydia stowed the milk, salad and lasagne in the fridge and left the rest of the bag on the counter in the tiny kitchen. She flicked the switch on the kettle and went to the living room to face Fleet.

He was standing in the bay window, looking down at the

117

street outside. The sun decided to come out at that moment and lit up his face.

'I can do tea or coffee, but it's instant. The coffee, not the tea. The tea is teabags.' Lydia pressed her lips together to stop any more words from spilling out. Fleet looked impossibly large in this room and she was regretting bringing him up. She had thought to keep him away from Charlie's cafe, but now she wondered if this was worse. Letting him behind the curtain, so to speak. It was all very well for Charlie to say 'don't go to the cops' but what did you do when they came to you? And then stood in your bare and sad temporary living space making everything look even uglier in comparison.

'Nothing for me, thanks,' Fleet said. He had his hands behind his back. 'I'll do the work bit, first.'

'All right,' Lydia said. 'Have a seat.'

Fleet sat in the middle of the sofa, his arms resting on his knees, hands clasped. He looked serious and Lydia felt a thrill of fear.

'John Smith is dead.'

'What?' Lydia felt her legs go wobbly. There wasn't another chair so she sank to the floor and sat cross-legged.

'He went into cardiac arrest late last night.'

'But he was awake, wasn't he? I thought you spoke to him?'

Fleet shook his head. 'Only briefly and not for a while. He landed feet first, which was consistent with the pattern of his injuries. Turns out the impact to his head must have been worse than first thought. The swelling in his brain was so bad they had to induce a coma for twenty-four hours. They were trying to bring him out of it yesterday and, from what I can gather — lot of medical jargon and not a lot of straight-talking — but they seemed to think his state of unconsciousness was getting lighter. He had started to respond to motor stimulation.'

'He was coming round?'

'Apparently. Although nothing was for sure, of course.'

'And then he just died?' Lydia wondered if Jason was around, listening, and how he felt about committing manslaughter. She remembered John Smith's dead-eye look and hoped he felt just fine.

'Smith was breathing unaided, but he was in the ICU and hooked up to monitors. The alarm sounded at 1.27am and by 1.56 he was pronounced. The post-mortem should be today or tomorrow and that will shed some light.' He paused. 'Interestingly, there was a gap in the CCTV footage just before the alarm went off.'

Lydia commanded her face not to react.

Fleet didn't say anything for a few moments, just looked at her as if he was waiting for her to say something that he already knew. It was an excellent technique and expertly applied. Lydia had been on a course on interrogation and she brought the voice of the trainer to mind: 'Leave spaces for your interviewee to fill.' Well, Fleet was certainly doing that. Two could play at that game and Lydia pressed her lips together. Was it her imagination or were his eyes getting warmer? Were his pupils dilating? Was he interrogating her or looking lustful. She felt her face flush at this thought. To cover her confusion, she went on the offensive. 'Are you any closer to an ID? It's been days.'

Fleet shook his head. 'Nobody has been in touch, nobody visited him...' A beat. 'That we are aware of, anyway. Do you still think the attack was specifically targeted at you because of your family name?'

Lydia took her time before answering. He could spring questions on her all he liked, she wasn't just a trained investigator, she had grown up with Henry Crow for a father. A cop, even a good cop with distracting sex appeal on his side, couldn't compete. 'I'm not sure,' Lydia said, finally. 'As I said when I spoke to you before, it was just a feeling. Could be born of the panic of the situation. I just thought I should pass on all of my impressions.' She widened her eyes a little. 'Full disclosure.'

'Is that so,' Fleet said, a smile threatening to break through.

'So are you treating Smith's death as suspicious?'

'I'm treating everything about that man as suspicious,' Fleet said. 'There is something not right, there. The gap in the CCTV is suspicious, too, of course. We're looking into how that could happen.'

'Can I see him?'

'Sorry?'

The chances of Mr Carter tracking her to London for his little grudge match were practically non-existent and, while Lydia knew she was more than capable of pissing people off, she hadn't been in town long enough. Which meant John Smith had been sent by somebody else. Maybe a Fox-shaped somebody. She hadn't sensed any of the Families at the time, but it was possible she had been too frightened. 'John Smith. Can I see him?'

'You are the victim in an ongoing investigation, I'm not sure that's wise.'

'Maybe I could identify him.' Or maybe sense some magic like the good little machine she was.

Fleet's eyes narrowed. 'You said you didn't know him.'

'I don't think so, but it was super-scary.' Lydia shrugged. 'I know you're probably used to having your life threatened all the time, Fleet, but I'm not. I could barely see anything I was so scared. Maybe I was wrong.'

He paused. 'Leave it with me.'

'Great.' Too late, Lydia realised that she probably sounded too enthusiastic. Fleet would, if he hadn't already, come to the same conclusion as most people that she was an oddball. 'What was the personal reason?'

'Sorry?'

120

'You said this visit was fifty-fifty.' Lydia tried to ignore the way her heart had sped up.

'There can't be a personal reason,' Fleet said. 'Not officially.' He looked at her significantly, as if wishing he could say more.

'That doesn't make any sense.'

'You are the victim in an ongoing investigation. It is inappropriate for there to be any kind of personal contact between myself, the SIO on the case, and you. The victim.'

'Could you stop saying that?'

'What?'

'Victim.'

Fleet looked uncertain for the first time. 'Oh, right. Sorry. Yes.'

'So the personal business you wanted to discuss was the lack of personal business.'

'Yes,' Fleet said. 'I thought it was best to clear that up.'

'And you think that is what you're doing right now?' Lydia crossed her arms. 'Making things clearer?'

He shook his head. 'I don't know what I'm doing. I just thought I should say something... After I came round the other night. That was inappropriate. I don't know what I was thinking. I apologise.'

'Don't worry about it,' Lydia said. She felt a wave of something which felt like exhaustion. A moment later she identified it. Disappointment. He was a copper and was just making sure he hadn't stepped outside the rulebook. Or, more to the point, that she wouldn't make trouble for him for stepping outside the rulebook.

Fleet was at the door, now, making to leave.

'Close the front door firmly,' she said, formally releasing him from the suddenly awkward conversation.

'You should use the deadbolt.'

'Thank you for the advice,' Lydia said.

'Right. I'll go, then.' He nodded as if deciding something and then left.

Lydia listened to his footsteps on the stairs and, without thinking it through, found herself following. 'Fleet?'

He stopped, looking back up at her from halfway down the steps.

'Was the gap in the CCTV a clean jump-cut? Something edited out after the event?' Although why someone with that kind of access wouldn't just wipe the whole thing, Lydia didn't know.

For a moment Lydia wasn't sure if he was going to respond, but then he said: 'The footage went fuzzy for five minutes before the alarms went off. Like there was electrical interference or something.'

Charlie. Damn it.

CHAPTER TEN

The mortuary was in a modern annex at the back of the main hospital building. Lydia had never been into one, although she figured that she had seen enough death on television and film to know what to expect. Those creepy body drawers. Some rookie police officer throwing up in the corner. A creepy, over-enthusiastic technician.

Getting out of her ancient Volvo and ringing the buzzer on the nondescript doorway, a small NHS sign with the words 'Mortuary Services' the only indication that she was in the right place, Lydia felt the first stirrings of trepidation. She knew, logically, that there was no more reason for her to meet spirits in this place than any other – people had died, in great numbers, everywhere. Especially somewhere as highly populated and old as London. But still, there was nothing like slapping yourself in the face with mortality to bring on the superstitions.

The door opened. Instead of a technician or receptionist, it was Fleet. He was wearing a suit and had his wool coat draped over one arm. 'Right on time,' he said. 'You up for this?'

Lydia nodded. She was suddenly keenly aware of her

family name. She couldn't faint or get sick. She was Lydia Crow and the Crows did not flinch.

Inside, there was a small waiting room with padded chairs and a coffee table stacked with magazines. It was warm and there was a vase of fresh flowers on the reception desk and a board pinned with thank you cards in muted colours and adverts for local funeral homes.

They were met by a woman in green scrubs with a plastic apron over the top. 'This is Felicity Syed,' Fleet said. 'Felicity, this is Lydia Crow. Is it all right if she takes a look?'

Lydia didn't know whether to offer to shake hands but the moment passed and they were heading down an anonymous institutional corridor. And then, through a set of doors with a keypad lock, and into a gleaming white room which was suddenly cool after the warmth of the public area. Lydia's brain was trying to keep up with the surreal sight of four stainless steel tables, each with drainage holes and lights above.

'Here we go.' Felicity led them to the only occupied table. There was the shape of a body underneath a sheet and, for a split second, Lydia thought that she might just bail.

Felicity folded the sheet upwards, exposing feet, then legs and a torso and, eventually, a head. It was the man from her first night at The Fork. Lydia recognised him instantly, while her brain insisted that it wasn't a human being she was looking at. It wasn't a person, just a humanoid shape or a waxwork dummy. There was a smell, though, tickling the back of her nose and throat. Something meaty underneath the tang of disinfectant and ethanol.

'You recognise him?'

'Yes,' Lydia managed.

'You know who he is? A name?'

'No,' Lydia said. Under the sheet, the man was almost-naked. A green gown had been tucked around his mid-section, hiding his thighs, groin and lower abdomen. It looked grotesque, like he had wrapped a towel around himself after stepping from the shower. At the same time, Lydia was very glad he wasn't completely naked. His torso had several tattoos, all in black ink. Two eight-pointed stars, one below each collar bone, looked more rustic than the intricate image of Prometheus chained to a rock with the sea and a sailing boat in the background which covered his chest and stomach. There was a curling design around one wrist and Lydia leaned closer to see if there were letters in the pattern or whether it was familiar. The tattoos meant nothing to Lydia. She searched her mind, rifling through the family lore, magical incantations and gossip, the symbols associated with the four families, and the names of all her clients back in Aberdeen. Nothing.

Fleet was watching her intently. 'We've identified him as Artur Bortnik.'

'He's Russian?'

'You're surprised.'

'He didn't sound Russian. I would have told you if he'd sounded Russian.' Lydia looked at the man's feet. There was a small tattoo on his left foot. Another star. 'How did you know?'

'These,' Fleet pointed out the eight-pointed stars on the shoulders, 'indicate a professional criminal according to Russian prison tradition.'

'What about this?' Lydia pointed at the Greek mythology.

'The chains and ship are probably meant to signal that he can or has escaped prison and that he is willing to travel for his work.'

Lydia couldn't stop staring at Bortnik. 'Why did you let me in here if you've already identified him?'

'We got a match through Interpol. Bortnik is a known associate of the Bratva. Don't know how deep he is connected, but he has been observed in the presence of some low-level members which was enough to win him a

125

place in the database.' Fleet dipped his chin, regarding her with brown eyes which were both concerned and suspicious. 'I wanted to check if this,' he indicated the dead Russian, 'would jog your memory at all.'

'No,' Lydia said. 'If I could remember anything else I would tell you.'

'And you can't think of any reason why the Bratva would know you?'

'I have no connections to the Russian Mafia,' Lydia said. The words were ridiculous. She had never even been to Russia.

'He's in pretty good shape, considering.' Fleet was mercifully no longer eye-balling her and had turned to the body. 'His top half, anyway.'

Lydia kept her lips tightly clamped. Suddenly the urge to throw up had become very insistent and she could feel prickles of sweat breaking out across her forehead and the back of her neck.

Felicity, who had been standing at a discreet distance and studying something on a tablet, stepped forward and pulled the sheet back over the Russian's torso and head. 'You need to sit down?'

Lydia gave a small head shake. Her hearing had gone echoey and strange and there was darkness crowding around the edges of the room.

'Sit,' Felicity said, steering Lydia to a chair. She put a hand on the back of Lydia head and pushed. 'Head down.'

Within moments, Lydia's hearing returned to normal. She sat up.

'Slowly,' Felicity said.

'This must happen all the time,' Lydia said, feeling like an idiot.

'Come on,' Fleet said, looking guilty. 'I'll buy you lunch.'

'I'm not hungry,' Lydia said, but she was grateful for the excuse to leave the hospital.

THE CAFE HAD red awnings and bistro tables on the pavement outside. The part of Lydia that wasn't still feeling sick was curious as to what kind of cafe the enigmatic copper would favour. She was pleased that it was a traditional Italian joint with decent coffee and a non-pretentious, non-annoying menu. Inside there were wooden beams on the low ceiling and an assortment of attractive bric-a-brac on shelves like rusting metal weighing scales, old glass bottles, and creamy plaster cherubs.

At a cosy table in a quiet corner, with her back to the wall and a good view of the place, Lydia felt some of the knots in her shoulders and neck ease. She couldn't keep walking around with this much tension, she knew, and the sight of her attacker laid out on the metal table ought to have been a relief. He couldn't come after her again. She was safe. The words rang hollow.

Fleet returned from the counter with a couple of menus and two glasses of water.

'You're frowning again.'

'Thinking,' Lydia said, remembering what Jason had said about her being scary and trying to smooth out her expression.

'I figured.' Fleet turned his attention to the menu and Lydia took the opportunity to look at him, unobserved for a moment.

The problem she realised, was that knowing one man was dead did not help as she didn't know who he was or what he wanted. If he was a one-off nut job, fine. She was safe. But finding out he was a professional was far worse. 'You said the stars indicated a professional criminal.'

Fleet looked up. 'They were done in prison. A tradition to sort out the hierarchy inside.'

'I thought they looked more home-made than the others.'

127

'There were more on his back, too. A knife dripping blood.'

Lydia's mouth had gone dry but she forced out a single word. 'Charming.'

'More code. It indicates a killer for hire. The number of drops of blood are the number of hits already performed.'

'Performed,' Lydia echoed. She felt utterly nauseated, now. A professional hit man had to have been sent by somebody. Who the hell could hate her that much, already?

Fleet tapped her menu. 'You know what you want?'

Lydia turned her attention to the laminated sheet. Her appetite was nowhere to be seen. Lydia considered her strong stomach a point of pride, but she couldn't fake it. 'I'm not hungry. Which is weird because I'm *always* hungry. Always.'

'It's okay,' Fleet said. 'How about the parmigiana? The garlic focaccia is really good here.'

Lydia nodded, trying the fact that her stomach had just taken a dive for the floor. 'And a coke.' Perhaps the sugar would sort her out.

Fleet went to order at the counter and Lydia tried to focus on the exceptional rear view of DCI Fleet rather than the churning shock and fear. A hit man. A hit. Somebody ordering her death like they were choosing an option on a menu. 'Some garlic focaccia and end Lydia's life, please.' Just like that. Her mouth filled with saliva and she focused on DCI Fleet instead, watching him walk back across the cafe.

Of course, focusing on Fleet only led to another problem. He wasn't going to have anything to do with her because she was part of an on-going investigation. Plus, and this thought had come rather slowly, he was a copper and she was a Crow. She might be a poor excuse for one, but it still counted.

'I'm sorry about that,' Fleet said, putting down their drinks and a wooden spoon with a table number on it.

'Don't tell me they've run out of the focaccia.' Lydia put a hand to her chest in mock horror.

'No,' his lips lifted into a quick smile. 'I shouldn't have shown you Bortnik.'

'It's okay. It was good to be sure.' Lydia didn't realise the truth of the words until they left her mouth.

He nodded, like he understood. 'He can't come after you again.'

'I just wish I knew whether he was working for someone else. Or what he wanted with me.'

Fleet leaned back but he was watching her carefully. 'You really don't know anything?'

'I really don't,' Lydia said, concentrating on the task of pouring cola into a glass. 'I'll ask my boss at the agency, but I've tried to think of any possible Russian connections to any of the jobs that I worked and there's nothing. And I've never had anything to do with the Bratva. Which is not something I expected to have to state.'

'He had very low-level connections years ago. He's not necessarily part of the organisation, now. He's over here, for starters. And has clearly been travelling for his work. I think it's more likely that he's just a contractor. Work for hire.'

'Just,' Lydia said. 'That's not as comforting as you might think.'

'What about since you came home? Can you think of anything that might have sparked this?'

Lydia thought about correcting him. Camberwell wasn't home, not for her. She had been brought up in the leafy suburbs, never feeling like she fitted in and resentful of the city-life and the magical family she was missing. Then she'd moved around, always looking for somewhere which felt like home and never finding it. 'I had literally just arrived,' she said instead. 'I hadn't had time to get into any trouble.'

Fleet nodded but his face told a different story.

'What?' Lydia said. 'Spit it out.'

'Your family.'

'I told you before, I don't have anything to do with the Crow Family. I'm a lame duck. A spare part.'

He frowned. 'Except you are living above The Fork. That's been in the Crow Family since I was a kid. And your uncle –'

'My uncle is just my uncle. The cafe isn't open. I'm staying for a couple of weeks. That's it. All there is to it.' Lydia wondered if the Silver Family were right and words were magic. She wondered if she kept on saying it, she could make it true.

'I'm going to ask a couple of uniforms to keep an eye on your place.' Fleet took a tip of his espresso.

Lydia opened her mouth to tell him not to do her any special favours, that she was completely fine and a Crow, which gave her all the protection she would ever need.

'It's not negotiable, so don't even try,' Fleet said, glaring at her over the rim of his coffee cup.

'Thank you,' Lydia said and watched his smile break out like sunshine.

CHAPTER ELEVEN

Lydia woke up in the plain bedroom and drank the lukewarm can of cola she had left by her bed the night before. Daylight was slanting through the gap in the thin curtains, slicing a hot white line across the duvet. The breakfast cola and lack of décor was depressing and Lydia found herself wondering whether she ought to buy a lamp for the room. She grabbed her phone from the floor and checked her messages and Maddie's social media accounts, before the madness could fully take hold. There was no need to beautify the room because she wasn't going to be staying. She would be back in her own home before she knew it.

Emma had responded, finally, to her text messages. Not via SMS but on WhatsApp. A picture of Emma's kitchen table covered in rainbow-striped paper plates overflowing with fairy cakes and sandwiches, toys, popped balloons, and scrunched-up paper napkins covered in unidentifiable food gunk.

Lydia typed. 'Shit. I've missed a birthday, haven't I? Sorry for being such a crap friend.'

She hesitated. Was it better or worse to admit that she had no idea whether it was Archie or Maisie's birthday she

131

had missed? Then typed: 'Will make it up to both of you. Promise.'

CHARLIE WAS WATCHING Madeleine's credit card accounts and the GPS on her phone in case anything pinged. Nothing. Lydia lay back and stared at the ceiling while she thought. Where would a rich girl go without using her cards or withdrawing cash? To a friend or boyfriend. Of course, Madeleine could be using a fake identity if she'd worked out a whole escape plan in advance. She had the funds for good documents and she was a Crow which meant she had the contacts, too. Even Lydia, having been brought up in a safe suburbia, officially 'out' of the business, knew that the best forger worked out the back of a launderette on Well Street.

Which naturally led to the perplexing question of 'why'. Maddie lived a charmed life. Doted-on Crow daughter, shiny-looking friends with expensive handbags and manicured nails, more money than any nineteen year old should have, and a job in her profession of choice. There were three areas to look into. Verity from the email who was 'sorry about how things worked out', Paul Fox and his bloody animal magnetism, and Minty PR.

Lydia hauled herself upright and pulled on yesterday's clothes. Once she had coffee she sat cross-legged on the sofa and opened her laptop. Verity had used a gmail account, not a work one, but the tone of the email suggested work colleague or acquaintance rather than friend.

Next, she made an appointment to see the boss at Minty PR. She knew the next logical step was to get in touch with Paul Fox but she no longer had his mobile number and knew that even if she had, it would almost certainly have changed. Lydia drained her coffee while pretending she wasn't relieved about this. She was still going to have to find the man and speak to him. It was a stay of execution, not a total reprieve.

Lydia flexed her fingers and held them poised about the keyboard, ready to begin the Fox hunt when the door buzzed. Lydia froze. Then she forced herself to relax. Angel was downstairs in the café and had probably come up to ask her something. Or it was Uncle Charlie. Nobody else knew she was here and would have come straight up to the flat.

Wishing she had a spyhole or a safety chain, Lydia opened the door.

The Fox brother from the night outside the club was stood on her landing. 'Paul wants to see you.'

'That's handy,' Lydia said. She slipped a hand into her jacket pocket and closed her fingers around the can of illegal Mace she kept there.

'War Museum. Half an hour.'

He turned and walked down the stairs and Lydia watched him go before retreating inside and slamming her door. She took several deep breaths and then went downstairs to politely request that Angel didn't send random people up to her flat.

She found Angel sitting in one of the tables by the front window drinking a glass of orange juice and reading on a tablet.

'Opening this weekend,' Angel said, without looking up. 'Fair warning.'

'See that door,' Lydia waited until Angel raised her gaze and then pointed at the one she had just come through. 'Don't let people through it.'

Angel tilted her head without smiling. 'It's the customer toilets.'

'Right.' Lydia closed her eyes for a moment. Bloody Uncle Charlie and his café. 'That guy who just came up. He wasn't a customer. We're not even open, yet.'

'What guy?'

'Never mind.' Lydia gave up and went to get ready for her meeting. She would just have to get a better door for the flat, with a security chain and a deadbolt. And maybe a crossbow, too.

THE SUN WAS SHINING on the two battleship gun barrels which dominated the entrance to the museum and there were several visitors posing in front of them, smiling for their phone cameras. Lydia spotted Paul Fox immediately, a little off to one side, his back turned to her in a display of studied unconcern. He appeared to be alone but that didn't mean anything; Foxes were excellent at hiding.

Lydia walked up the middle of the wide gravel path. She wanted Paul to see that she was alone and that there was no need for panic. She wanted him to know that she had understood the unsubtle message coded in his choice of location.

Paul Fox turned when she was about ten feet away, smiling at her like she was dessert. He looked just as incredible as Lydia remembered and was wearing a fitted black T-shirt and black jeans. It was the exact outfit she had last seen him in five years ago and she knew that was no accident.

'Lydia Crow in the flesh. I heard you had flown back to the nest.'

'Not as such,' Lydia said.

Paul continued as if she hadn't spoken. 'I didn't really believe it. You said you were done with London.' He waved a hand. 'Where was it you flew off, too? Siberia?'

'Scotland,' Lydia said.

Paul smiled. 'Well, you look good. Moving away was obviously the right thing. Makes me wonder why you'd do something as stupid as come back.'

Lydia relaxed. Hostility she could deal with. 'Did you want to go inside? Brush up on your history?'

134

Paul's smile grew wider. He nodded toward the green space of the park. 'Thought we could take a seat in the fresh air.' He drew a flat metal flask out of his back pocket. 'Have a nip of this while we catch up.'

Lydia shook her head. 'Bit early for me.'

'You never used to be so cautious.'

'Older and wiser,' Lydia said.

'So,' Paul took a swig from the flask and then put it away. 'I assume you were sniffing around my club looking for the pleasure of my company. Feeling nostalgic?'

'Madeleine Crow.' Lydia had considered the subtle approach but faced with Paul Fox's smug face, she had thrown that out of the window. She watched him carefully. Not to see if he was lying, that was a given, but to look for the kernel of truth or the important lie which might lead Lydia somewhere useful.

'I bought you something,' Paul said. 'A welcome-home gift. It's being delivered to your place right now.'

Lydia wanted to ask how he and his family knew where 'her place' was, but she clamped her lips together. She wasn't going to give him the satisfaction.

Paul tilted his head, appraising. Her senses were filled with the unmistakable Fox tang. She wished she could dial down her ability at will so that it didn't always have to be so overwhelming. Yes, it's a Fox, she told her body. You can stop letting me know.

'Madeleine Crow,' she said, again. 'Don't pretend you don't know her, you were observed leaving a club together.'

'So you're an investigator, now,' Paul said. 'I might have some work for you.'

'I'm just doing a favour,' Lydia said. 'I'll be out of here soon enough.'

Paul shook his head. 'What better place to ply your trade? You know people. Or you soon will. You'll get clients, like that.' He clicked his fingers.

Lydia opened her mouth to tell him that she only had one year's experience and was in no position to start her own agency but then she remembered who he was and that this wasn't a friendly chat.

'There's a little matter I could book you for.'

'Wife cheating on you?' Lydia said quickly, trying to regain control of the conversation.

He just smiled. 'Still a merry bachelor.'

'Well, I'm not looking for work and I won't be in London for long,' Lydia said. 'And we were talking about Madeleine.'

'I know Maddie,' Paul said. 'Nice girl.'

'Do you know where she is?'

'Nah,' Paul shook his head. 'I heard she'd gone missing, though. Careless, that. Charlie needs to take better care of his fledglings.'

'Is that a threat?' Lydia forced her voice to remain even. In her memory Paul Fox had been all charm and affection. She had known he was a Fox and had seen him use cold words and sly looks on other people, but when he had turned to her he had been all warmth and security, but in a safe, restrained kind of a way. Gallant. With hindsight, he had been playing a part that was perfect for the nervous and inexperienced nineteen year old she had been. Her eyes were clearer, now. Or he was playing a different role. Either way, every molecule in Lydia's being was telling her to get out of the park and as far away from Paul Fox as possible.

'If you know something, you need to tell me.' Lydia reached a hand into her jacket pocket, curled her fingers around a coin and used it to centre her feelings. 'Better me than Charlie.'

'Is that so?' Paul looked away down the path, watching the people walking past. 'Things aren't what they used to be, little bird. You should find out the lay of the land before you start throwing your name around.'

'Why don't you tell me the lay of the land?' Lydia said. 'I'd love to learn.'

Paul stopped studying the crowd and turned back to Lydia. 'You will.' He moved quickly, grabbing her roughly by the shoulders and kissing her on the lips in a distinctly un-gallant manner. His mouth pushed at hers, a tongue attempted to thrust inside. Lydia ignored the urge to pull away and, instead, leaned in, raising her knee at the same time so that it connected with a soft part of Paul Fox. He folded and Lydia moved neatly away.

'Don't do that again,' she said and then walked away.

AFTER A LATE LUNCH and a long walk to settle her nerves, Lydia got off the Northern Line at Oval and headed above ground. As soon as mobile reception kicked in, her phone began ringing. Fleet.

'What's up, officer?' Lydia was more happy to hear from him than she cared to admit.

'Just checking in.'

'Checking up on me?' Lydia began walking home. A big guy with a long platinum blonde wig, sandals and a Jesus-style white robe was walking toward her on the pavement and she took a moment to cross to the other side of the road. There was good-crazy, fun-crazy, and bad-crazy, and after her meeting with Paul Fox, Lydia wasn't in the mood for any crazy at all.

She lost Fleet's voice as she navigated the traffic. 'Sorry, what did you say?'

'Are you okay? After Bortnik. I shouldn't have shown you –'

'I'm fine,' Lydia said. 'I told you.'

'I want you to be careful,' Fleet's voice was still concerned. 'Don't take unnecessary risks.'

'Everybody seems to have advice for me today,' Lydia

said. 'Any reason you are taking a special interest, DCI Fleet?'

There was a short silence. Then Fleet said, 'I think you can guess.'

'Because I'm a Crow?'

'Not everything is about that, you know,' Fleet said.

Lydia opened her mouth to ask him 'what, then?' but suddenly she felt heat in her face. Was he flirting with her?

'Anyway,' Fleet said, suddenly formal. 'Have a good evening.'

'What?' Lydia said, but he had already gone. Lydia put her phone back into her pocket and dodged around a crowded bus stop. The sight of The Fork coming into view, pushed Fleet momentarily from her mind. The cafe lights were on, making the place look like a beacon in the dark. Lydia didn't like it. She wanted quiet and anonymous.

Lydia unlocked the front door. There was a new sign hanging in the glass which was turned 'closed' side out. Angel was sitting at one of the tables out front, working through a plate of pastries and reading a book. 'What are you doing?'

Angel took her time, licking her fingers and putting her book face down on the table before replying. 'Isn't it obvious?'

'Here, I mean,' Lydia said. 'It's late. Why don't you go home?'

'Nat has band practice. It's too noisy.'

'Nat?'

Angel gave her a withering look. 'My wife.'

Lydia paused at the door to upstairs. She wanted to say 'you can't use The Fork as an extension to your living room' but she didn't quite dare. Angel had... Presence.

'Night,' she said instead. 'Can you lock up when you leave?'

Angel had picked up her book again and ignored her.

Lydia trudged up the stairs to the flat. At the top of the stairs she stopped.

When she had left earlier to meet Paul Fox, the front door to her flat had been an off-white B&Q special. That had gone. In its place was a rich brown wooden door with a panel of obscured glass in the top half. Bronze leaf lettering in a vintage-looking font with a drop-shadow were the words: Crow Investigations.

Lydia stared at the new door. It was ridiculous and it was gorgeous. Finally, she took her phone out of her pocket and called Charlie. 'Did you put a new door in the flat?'

'No. Why, do you want one?'

'No. Never mind.' She hung up before he could ask for a progress report and opened the new door, poised on the balls of her feet to run. The living room was empty and just as she had left it. The only evidence that anyone had been there was a small pile of wood dust from a drill and, of course, the new door.

She walked through the rest of the flat, checking, then went into the living room and sat on the sofa. With the living room door open, she could see straight down her hallway and had a perfect view of the new addition. Numb surprise gave way to fury and she stood up, fists clenching. Perhaps there was a hammer somewhere in the building. Smashing it would be cathartic. Of course, then she wouldn't have a front door at all.

Her mobile began playing The White Stripes. Unknown number.

'Yes?' Lydia rubbed little circles into her right temple, trying to ease her headache.

His voice, insufferably confident brought with it the unmistakable tang of Fox. 'Do you like your present?'

'You fucker,' Lydia said. 'You think this is funny? What the hell do you think you're playing at?'

'Hey, little bird, that's no way to show gratitude.'

139

Lydia was pacing the room as she spoke, the anger really flowing now. It was reckless to shout at a Fox but she no longer cared. 'You don't give me gifts. We are not together.'

'You like it, though, right? That retro style to go with your retro attitude and your retro home. You do know it's okay to move on? That cafe looks like it hasn't been touched since the sixties.'

'Next time you want to waste your money, just wire cash straight to my account.'

Paul ignored her. 'Charlie hankering after the good old days? Trying to get something started with his little bird nesting in The Fork.'

Lydia stopped pacing and let out a silent breath. Paul was fishing. 'Forget Charlie. You do not send me things. We are not friends. We are not an item. We are nothing.'

'So how do I still know you so well?' Paul said. 'Admit it, you like your present. I know you better than you know yourself. I know what you want.' His voice dropped lower. 'I know what you need.'

'You need to think very carefully before you start something with me,' Lydia said. Her senses were screaming 'Fox!' and she wished they would quiet down and let her think.

'I remember,' Paul said. 'You hurt my feelings earlier.'

'You do not come to my home. You do not send people to my home. Stay out of my way.'

'You want to avoid me?' Paul's voice had lost its smile. 'Fly away, little bird. Fly away fast.'

Lydia dropped the phone and closed her eyes for a moment. When she opened them again, the door was still there.

Lydia found the bourbon and splashed some into her empty coffee mug. She stared at the door and willed the alcohol to take the edge off her feelings. It was unnerving how well Paul could guess her desires. It was something he had always been good at and it was horrible to discover that he still had the knack. Unless it was coincidence. His plans had simply happened to align with her deepest hopes and dreams. Crow Investigations. It had a ring to it. And she would be her own boss. Lydia knocked back the last of the bourbon. She shouldn't even think about it. It was madness.

Still. The letters seemed to glow... Invitingly.

CHAPTER TWELVE

Minty PR was in Soho down one of the cobbled side-streets with wrought iron railings and geometric planters filled with cutting-edge topiary and thin young people dressed in black. Lydia also favoured dark colours but her clothes were battered and old and she knew she stuck out amongst the shiny happy creatives. That suited her just fine, though. She slouched into the reception of Minty and leaned on the desk to give her name. A man with sculpted facial hair offered her coffee and said, apologetically enough, that Harry was running late. Lydia took her coffee and wandered around the room, studying the campaigns and awards displayed on the walls and the glossy brochures. The firm's clients included car manufacturers, a national coffee-shop chain, and a government health initiative. The office wasn't as large as she expected, either, and when Harry ushered her back to his domain he seemed genuinely willing to help. 'I'm so sorry about Madeleine,' he said. 'It was just awful.'

'Thank you,' Lydia said. 'Wait, what was awful?'

Harry looked confused. 'Letting her go. We didn't want

to, absolutely not, but it was a difficult situation and we felt... Well. We really didn't have a choice.'

'You fired her?' Lydia decided to act ignorant in the hope that Harry would give her as many details as possible. Karen had always said that people just loved to educate, you just had to give them the chance.

Harry spread his hands. 'We're really sorry. I am happy to give her a reference. I told her that at the time.'

'What happened?'

Harry frowned. 'You don't know?'

'I want to hear your side of the story,' Lydia said. 'My uncle, Charlie, was very upset.'

Harry went to speak but Lydia leaned forward. 'Between you and me, he's a bit blind when it comes to family. I know Maddie could be handful, but Charlie,' she shook her head, 'he wouldn't have it.'

'He didn't believe me,' Harry said. 'I could tell.'

'He's protective,' Lydia said. 'I just want to find out the truth of it, though.'

'Why?'

Lydia smiled. 'I'm family and I run a business which means there is every chance I'll get saddled with providing gainful employment for my delightful cousin any day now. I just want to know what I'm in for.' Harry didn't seem to know that Madeleine was missing and Lydia saw no reason to tell him.

Harry was visibly relaxing as he realised that Lydia hadn't arranged the meeting in order to shout at him. Lydia could well imagine how his meeting with Charlie had gone. 'She's a great girl,' Harry said. 'Woman, I mean. Sorry.'

Lydia nodded and sipped her coffee.

'But she was erratic. Our internships are highly prized, we have loads of excellent applicants and they are way over-qualified for the stuff they end up doing but it's the way we all started, you know? You have to pay your dues in this business.'

Lydia could imagine the drill. Bright young things photocopying and fetching coffee.

'Do you know the most important thing in PR?'

'Getting press?' Lydia said.

'Making the client happy.' Harry smiled and Lydia felt herself warming to him, no wonder he had gone into this line of work. 'Frankly, that's the only thing that matters. You can run a shit campaign and your coverage can bomb, but you can blame a million other things for that. It's alchemy, you know, nobody knows why some things work and some things don't. Trying to capture public attention, trying to sway public opinion, it's like catching lightning in a bottle.'

Bollocks, Lydia thought, hoping it wasn't obvious that her bullshit meter was sounding a loud alarm.

Harry grinned. 'As long as the client likes you they will swallow anything. As long as they are happy you can sell them any result.' He dipped his head. 'Well, almost.'

Lydia smiled. It sounded a bit like PI work. Often the client knew exactly what you were going to find out. The result wasn't the most important thing, it was the way you delivered the news. Karen had been really good at that. Lydia, not so much. One of her 'learning points' had been to work on her charm. 'This isn't The Maltese Falcon,' Karen had said. 'People don't want hard-boiled, they want soft soap. Half of this job is counselling. I swear to God.' Then she would slide open her desk drawer and retrieve a half-smoked joint. Karen always accompanied training sessions with getting lightly stoned. 'It's the only way to get through the tedium,' she would say, having presumably used up all of her charm and patience on the clients. Lydia basically wanted to be Karen when she grew up.

'Client is king, got it.'

'And Maddie was great to start with. Vivacious. Pretty.'

He pulled an apologetic face. 'I'm not supposed to say that, I know.'

Lydia waved a hand to indicate that she didn't care. 'So what went wrong? She slept with the wrong person?'

Harry shook his head, suddenly very serious. 'You really don't know?'

'I don't.'

There was a pause while Harry was clearly weighing up his words. Finally, he said: 'She nearly killed a client.'

Lydia stamped on the urge to laugh. It was so ridiculous. So over dramatic. 'She did what? Spilled hot coffee in someone's lap? Tripped someone by accident? Slapped some guy for squeezing her arse?'

'It's really not a laughing matter.'

'Tell me.' Lydia flipped open her notebook.

'You can't write this down,' Harry said. His eyes flicked to the door. 'Your uncle made it all go away. I'm not supposed to talk about it to anyone, though. I know you're his niece, otherwise I wouldn't have said anything. I thought you knew. Wait-' he looked stricken. 'Was this a test? I swear I wouldn't say anything else.' The smooth PR facade had completely fallen away, now, and Harry was sweating.

'I swear I'm not here from my uncle. Nothing you say will get back to him. I'm looking for Madeleine, that's all.'

'Looking for her?'

'She's missing,' Lydia said. 'So just tell me what happened and I'll get out of here.' She closed her notebook. 'No notes.'

'Missing. Jesus.' Harry closed his eyes. 'That is bad.'

'I know,' Lydia said. 'I just want to find her. Make sure she's all right. Please.'

Harry swallowed but Lydia could see he wanted to talk. People usually did.

'It was really weird,' Harry said. 'Like I said, she started out fine, but she seemed to change. She wasn't smiling as much and she seemed kind of out of it a lot of the time. I wondered if she was on something.'

'Drugs?'

'Not coke. Something depressive like too much weed. Or I figured she was going through some personal shit. I had a friend who started therapy and he went really downhill for a few months before he picked up. It was like a psychological cleanse, like all the toxins had to come out before he could get better.'

'She seemed down?'

'More angry than sad, but that can happen.'

Lydia had spent a good part of her teens and early twenties feeling like she wanted to set fire to the world, so she could relate.

'Ivan Gorin owns Dean Street House.' Harry clocked Lydia's blank expression. 'The members' club.'

'Ah. Right.'

'You're thinking they don't need PR, right?'

'Uh-huh,' Lydia said, covering the fact that she had been desperately trying to place the name.

'Well, Gorin was planning to open a new restaurant next door. It was going to trade on the name, but not be members-only. He booked us to handle the launch because we're local.'

Lydia tried to look impressed.

'We were at a pre-opening taster night. Gorin wanted to test the menu. Wanted to test everything, actually, the guy's a complete control freak.'

'Why was Maddie there? Wasn't she just an intern?'

'He met her at the office one day and gave her an invite.' Harry shrugged. 'She's a nice-looking girl.'

'Woman,' Lydia corrected.

'Yes, sorry. Right.' Harry leaned forward. 'We had just had the intermezzo sorbet and I was watching Ivan because he'd been getting very friendly with Madeleine all evening.

He was a bit over-familiar with the female staff, especially after a few drinks, so I was watching out for her.' He shook his head. 'Next thing, the dessert is being served and Ivan and Madeleine have gone.'

'Gone?'

'I didn't realise at the time, but she had taken him to the bathroom. Presumably he thought he was getting lucky.'

'So, what happened?'

'I have no idea. When Ivan didn't show for a while, I went looking. Found him on the floor of the gents, white as death with blue lips.' Harry was staring, eyes wide like he was reliving the moment. 'Seriously, I thought he was dead. It was horrible.'

'But he was alive?'

Harry nodded tightly. 'I thought I was going to have to do CPR but when I got close, I could feel a little breath coming through his mouth and his colour started to improve. A bit, I mean, he still looked like shit.'

'And where was Madeleine? Was she there?'

'No. She must have gone out through the kitchens or something.' Harry shook his head, remembering. 'I had my phone out, but Ivan grabbed my hand. He was squeezing really tightly and like, staring. He tried to speak but it was just this whistling sound so I leaned in close and he managed to whisper 'no police'.'

'So you didn't call them?'

'He's the client and if he didn't want police, that was his call. Police would mean the press and I got it. I mean, it would be embarrassing for him.'

'And you didn't know if he'd done something illegal, like maybe he had tried to force himself on Madeleine and you were protecting your client.'

'It's my job,' Harry said. 'But I'm not stupid. I knew who Madeleine was so I called Charlie. He came right away.'

'Wait,' Lydia held up a hand. 'You called Charlie. Charlie Crow?'

Harry nodded. 'He came straight away.'

Lydia kept her expression neutral while her mind whirled. Why the hell hadn't Charlie told her about this incident? It seemed somewhat pertinent, which led to the next rational thought; what else wasn't her uncle telling her? 'Was Ivan recovering at this point?'

'Yeah, he was sitting up by the time your uncle arrived. He could whisper more clearly and his lips weren't blue anymore. He didn't want anyone to know, said I had to go out and make up something to tell the party. I said that he and Madeleine had gone off for some quiet time. Don't be cross,' he held up his hands. 'I made a nod-nod-wink-wink kind of thing. You know, randy old Ivan was less embarrassing than flat-out on the toilet floor Ivan. He's a very proud man.'

'And you wanted to keep his business.'

'Of course. And stop him from suing us over Madeleine or bad-mouthing the agency.'

'But you didn't call an ambulance?'

'I do as I'm told,' Harry said. 'When it comes to clients like Ivan Gorin, anyway.'

Money talked, as always.

'So, where was Madeleine?'

'I don't know. And I haven't seen her since. Thought she might call to apologise or send an email or something.'

'How did you fire her if you haven't seen her?'

'Sent an email and a letter. Left a message on her mobile. Trust me, she got the message.'

'But she didn't respond?'

'Nope.' He shifted in his seat. 'Are we done here?'

'What did Charlie do when he arrived that night?'

'I have no idea. I got out of there and went to do damage control in the restaurant.'

'Did Ivan speak to his guests?'

'No. I think he and Charlie went out the back way. Or maybe there's a connecting door between the properties and he went back that way to his club to recuperate.'

'And you've seen him since?'

Harry hesitated. 'Yes.' A moment more as confusion danced across his face. 'I think so.'

Lydia raised an eyebrow and waited.

'Actually,' Harry continued, 'now you mention it, I'm not sure if I've actually seen him. I've spoken to him on the phone, though. Definitely.'

'You're still the PR firm for Dean Street House?'

Harry swelled with pride. 'Naturally. We know how to do our job.'

CHAPTER THIRTEEN

Dean Street House wasn't far from Minty PR and Lydia figured that Ivan's loyalty was less to do with Harry's outstanding firm and more to do with convenience. The club had an unassuming entrance and Lydia was only certain that she had the right place because of the restaurant next door. On the other side was a juice bar with an editing studio above.

Lydia hit the intercom which buzzed loudly. 'Yes?'

'I'm here to see Ivan Gorin,' Lydia said. She held her business card up to the camera and smiled.

There was another buzzing sound and then a click. Lydia opened the door and found herself in a hallway with black and white tiles and painted panelling on the walls. An oak staircase was straight ahead and, next to a console table, there were several umbrellas in a stand. It was like a fancy-but-normal entrance to a family home and Lydia had a moment of uncertainty that she had the right place.

A startlingly thin woman descended the staircase, her fingers trailing the banister. She smiled at Lydia with all the warmth of an ice floe. 'May I help you?'

'I need to speak with Ivan. Is he here?'

'Sadly, you just missed him.'

'Fine. Give me his number and I'll call him.'

'I'm not at liberty to give out Mr Gorin's contact details, but you can send any media requests via his management.'

'I just came from his management and I heard a very interesting story about Ivan that I wish to discuss. Trust me, he'll want to talk to me in person. In private.' Lydia held out her card and watched as the woman glanced at it. If the name 'Crow' meant anything to her, Lydia couldn't tell.

'I will pass on the message, but you really are better off making contact via his management.'

'Tell him he needs to get in touch urgently. It is truly in his best interests.'

The woman had already turned away, had a foot on the bottom step.

'Thanks for being so helpful,' Lydia said. 'I'll be sure to let Ivan know you were a peach.'

LYDIA'S PHONE buzzed on her way out of Dean Street House. It was a text message from Emma and Lydia felt herself tense as if for a blow as she tapped the screen. 'Are you free? Coffee?' The tension flowed out and Lydia realised just how worried she had been that she had irrevocably upset Emma. The thought that she might lose her friendship had been too awful to look at head-on. She tapped back. 'Definitely! In Soho but can meet wherever – you at home?'

The sun was out by the time Lydia got onto the street, like it was echoing the boost in mood Emma's message had delivered. Another text pinged. 'Mum has the kids and I'm at the Mothership. Meet you outside?'

'Be there in twenty mins.'

Emma had always loved design and had been a homely sort, even when they were teens. She couldn't walk past a cushion without squeezing it and she and Lydia had spent many happy hours wandering around Liberty department store, gazing at the beautiful clothes and jewellery, the sumptuous fabrics and rugs, and day-dreaming of when they would be adults. Lydia always saw herself swanning around in one of the peacock-patterned silk robes, with a variety of gentlemen callers. Emma kept a binder of interior design ideas ready for when she had a home of her own.

Lydia walked fast toward Great Marlborough Street where Liberty sat in all its black-and-white timbered glory, and tried not to think about how far away from the ideal her life had veered. At least Emma had a home and family and was happy. Her perfect linen cushions tended to have rice cakes mashed into them these days, but Lydia knew Emma wouldn't have things any other way.

Emma was outside, as promised, wearing cropped jeans, a floaty white top and enormous sunglasses. It was momentarily odd to see her without Maisie and Archie hanging off her arms and just with a small cross-body bag, not a rucksack full of baby-supplies. After they had hugged hello, they both spoke at once: 'I'm sorry.'

'What? No.' Emma shook her head. 'I'm sorry. I've been weird.'

'I scared you,' Lydia said, deciding to get it out in the open. Even a small rift from Emma had made Lydia realise something very important; she could not lose her friend. It was unthinkable.

Emma didn't say anything, but she reached for Lydia and hugged her tightly.

'I'm sorry,' Lydia said into her friend's hair.

'Don't be.' Emma pushed her sunglasses up and fixed Lydia with a steady look. 'It's me. You just have to be honest with me. Don't shut me out.'

'Okay,' Lydia said, mentally filing that idea under 'crazy talk'. She turned and they began walking back toward the

153

tube. 'What do you fancy doing with your freedom? Food? Drinks?'

'I was thinking more investigating,' Emma said. 'Unless your cousin has turned up?'

Lydia shook her head. 'No.'

'To which?'

'Both,' Lydia said. 'I'm not freaking you out.' *Or putting you in danger.*

Emma stopped walking. 'I thought I made myself very clear. You have to open up. You've always been cagey about your family and I understand, but you're my best friend and we're not kids anymore. I need you to be honest with me.'

'I am being honest,' Lydia said. 'I swear.'

'Right, then. Tell me about your Uncle Charlie. He's the head of the family, right?'

'Correct.'

'And it used to be your Granddad?'

'Grandpa Crow. Yes.'

'And is everyone in your family magic or is it just you?'

Lydia had been swigging from her water bottle and she nearly spat it out. A woman talking nineteen-to-the-dozen on her mobile clipped her on the shoulder as she moved around Lydia's suddenly immobile form.

'What?' Emma said, eyes wide and innocent.

'I need a drink,' Lydia said, wiping her chin and neck. 'A proper drink.' She caught Emma's expression and added, hurriedly, 'I will answer you.'

Emma seemed to take pity on Lydia. 'It's so nice out. We could go to that place in Russell Square gardens. Have a cheeky glass of white.'

They changed direction and headed towards Blooms-bury, and Lydia was glad when Emma allowed her to change the subject to Maisie and Archie. 'And how about Tom?' Lydia knew she didn't ask about Emma's husband often enough. It was yet another way in which she wasn't a great friend. She resolved, as she so often had, to do better.

'Yeah, he's good. You know Tom. Always chilled.'

When they reached Russell Square, Lydia cut through the park, towards the enormous Greek-revival monolith of The British Museum. 'How do you feel about some culture first?'

Emma blew out a sigh of exasperation and made a show of checking her watch. 'Fine,' she said. 'Forty-five minutes of history will give me an hour and a half of drinking wine in the sunshine and listening to all the secrets my best mate has been holding back for the past twenty years.'

LYDIA HADN'T BEEN to the museum in a few years, but she still remembered the way. Once they had passed the stone columns and under the carved pediment of the grand entrance, they entered the inner courtyard with its vast glass roof. It was, as ever, rammed with visitors and Lydia cut through the throng as quickly as possible, dragging Emma up to the third floor of the museum and into the cool calm of gallery forty-one.

The Wedgwood blue walls and shining glass cases transported Lydia back in time to visits with her Dad. While he had honoured his wife's wishes to bring Lydia up away from the modern-incarnation of the Family, he had still wanted her to know her own history. As a little girl, Lydia had accepted the stories as being not much different from her book of Grimm's fairy tales or the giant tome of Norse legends with the exploits of Loki. The last time she had been here, though, her Dad had opened up a little more about Grandpa and his memories of his mother, Great Grandma Crow. They had been standing in front of a Viking treasure hoard, dug up by some detectorists near York, when her Dad had pointed at a shining gold coin. It was a match for the one she always had at her fingertips. The Family coin that could be made to appear, disappear and spin in lazy circles. She felt a jolt of fury at it being entombed in the case, out of reach, away from human contact. Like it was a live thing and not a disc of metal.

'It's all right,' her father's hand was on her shoulder before Lydia realised that she was up to the case, hands splayed on the glass in direct disobedience of the printed signs. 'It's a replica.'

'What?' Lydia had dragged her gaze away and looked into her father's blue eyes.

'We switched it out while this hoard was being renovated ready for display.' The corners of his mouth lifted into a small smile.

Now, Lydia walked past the Viking hoard and the bronze ceremonial shield which, her Dad had told her had hidden inscriptions on the underside which had baffled the historians, but that any true Crow would be able to read if they found a need to do so. When her Dad spoke about their family history, it had been hard to know where myth ended and fact began and, Lydia admitted, it still was.

She stopped in front of the last cabinet in the room and touched Emma's arm. 'Look.'

The sword was only half-intact, having been broken sometime over the eleven centuries since it was made. The information card explained that the blade was pattern-welded iron with a five-lobed pommel, and was thought to have been found in the bed of the river Thames, left by an unknown Viking warrior. 'See the hilt,' Lydia said. 'There are remains of the gold inlay.'

Lydia knew what she was looking for but, even so, she thought the runic image of the crow was clear.

Emma wasn't saying anything and Lydia was about to explain when she said, 'is that a bird?'

'A crow,' Lydia said. 'We came over from Norway.'

Emma glanced at her. 'We?'

'This is the oldest artefact from our family collection.'

Emma frowned, reading the label out loud. 'Grip is tightly wound silver wire which, along with gold animal design, suggests a successful and wealthy individual.'

Lydia anticipated her question. 'The label doesn't name us because the curators don't know. Dad told me it was Finnr Hrōk.' Seeing Emma's blank expression she elaborated. 'Hrōk is Old Norse for rook or crow.'

Next, Lydia took Emma to the gallery for Europe in the 1600s. There was a gilt-brass watch-case from 1675, a complex design around the outside of the case of entwined leaves and branches. Framed by foliage, the silhouette of a bird. 'Crow family,' Lydia said, pointing to it.

'The label doesn't mention –' Emma began.

'I know,' Lydia cut her off. 'You wanted me to tell you, though, and this is what I know. Old objects, family lore, and a load of myths, which can't possibly be true.'

'Okay,' Emma said. Then, placating. 'It's very cool.'

'One more,' Lydia said, speed-walking through the galleries of glass cases, past stone statues and marble busts, ancient tapestries and intricate painted miniatures.

The gallery for 1900 to the present day was jarring after the earlier exhibits. In a few short minutes and after dodging around several tour groups and a class of school kids, talking at high volume, they had travelled from a world of pressed-metal weaponry and ancient bronze arm cuffs to an Art Deco television cabinet. 'How much do you know about the others?'

'The four families?' Emma said as they navigated the exhibits. 'There's Fox, Pearl, Crow and Silver.'

'Right,' Lydia said, stopping in front of a small stone fountain, mounted on a solid base. It had the City of London arms carved into the top section and had a pleasing, curved shape, but was otherwise quite plain. 'This was erected near St John's park in Westminster to commemorate the truce in 1943.'

'The truce?' Emma frowned. 'Was that to do with WWII?'

'Between the families. There had been all kinds of bad behaviour, fighting and power-grabs, and general mayhem. According to the stories, anyway. And this was back when we all had a fair amount of power.'

'Magic,' Emma said, eyes wide.

'Yeah. I guess. Special abilities. Whatever you want to call it.' This was why Lydia had always avoided talking about this stuff with Emma. She felt stupid saying fairytale words like 'magic' out loud. 'So, things were bad. People were dying on all sides and the heads of the families started discussing ways to stop it. There had been peace negotiations for a few years, but when the second world war kicked off, especially after the Blitz, there was renewed enthusiasm for banding together. Stronger together, patriotism, all that. They got together and made a pact to stay out of each other's way. Geographical areas of control and influence were allocated and everybody promised to leave each other's families alone.'

'What happened to it?'

'It's still holding,' Lydia said. Then, thinking about Maddie's disappearance. 'At least I hope it is.'

'I meant the fountain. It's cracked.'

'Oh, right.' Lydia nodded. 'There was a gas leak and it got demolished in the explosion. It was pieced back together and brought here for safe-keeping. Neutral ground.' She stepped closer and pointed out the carved symbols for the families. 'A pearl necklace for the Pearlies, the Silver family cup, the Fox head, and us,' Lydia stopped short of touching the stone, although her fingers ached to trace the image of the crow.

'So it's all true. I mean,' Emma waved her hands to

158

encompass the vast room, the crowds of visitors. 'We're in the British Museum.'

Lydia nodded. 'We got the City of London crest as a halfway measure to recognising status. I mean, there was talk about making one of the livery guild things, like the trades, but it was decided that a magical guild was a step too far. So we're sort of legit, sort of accepted as being real, but stopping just short of it. And now it doesn't really matter anymore. Silvers are still good at lying, but it's not like the old days. They can't talk you into jumping off the Gherkin anymore.'

'Jesus,' Emma said.

'Right?' Lydia was surprised at how much she was enjoying herself. Emma was hanging on her every word.

'Everyone says that the Crows were the strongest. Is that still the case?'

'Yeah,' Lydia's good mood evaporated instantly. 'I don't really know what that means, being brought up apart from them all. I'm in the dark.'

'You sound angry,' Emma said.

Lydia shrugged. 'It's just weird. You can't miss what you never had, but it feels like I failed a test I wasn't even given the chance to take –' She broke off as a pair of small dark-haired women wearing matching pink t-shirts and cropped jeans, stopped abruptly in front of her to take a selfie.

Once they had manoeuvred around the tourists, Emma put an arm around Lydia's waist and squeezed. 'Your mum and dad were just being protective.'

'I know,' Lydia said, leaning into Emma for a moment before breaking apart to let a tour group past.

They walked back through the gallery, heading to the exit. 'Look,' Emma stopped. 'More Crow stuff.'

'That's not ours,' Lydia said, taking an instinctive step back. 'At least, I don't think so. I hope not.'

It was a painting on a piece of parchment which looked

more like fabric than paper, lurking behind a protective sheet of glass. It was a stylised image of an enormous corvid. Its eyes round black holes and ragged wings spread.

'Nachtkrapp or Nattravnen.' Emma was leaning down, reading from the label.

'The night raven,' Lydia said, her throat dry. 'It's a bad omen. It doesn't have eyes, just tunnels. And if you look into its face, you die.'

Emma raised an eyebrow. 'Another lovely bedtime story? No wonder you went to Scotland.'

Lydia tried to smile.

'What is it,' Emma reached out.

'Nothing,' Lydia turned resolutely away from the painting. The Night Raven was just a myth. Brought over from Scandinavia centuries ago. *It can't hurt you*, Lydia told herself, but her feet sped up as she headed for the exit and she could hear Paul Fox's voice in her head: *Fly away little bird.*

CHAPTER FOURTEEN

After sinking a couple of bottles of red with Emma, Lydia was more than slightly tipsy. She squinted at her phone as she walked from the tube station back to the cafe. There was an email from Karen with the subject line 'Good News'. Mr Carter had been into the office to make a full apology. Apparently things were off again in his soap opera of a marriage and Karen wanted to know how soon Lydia could come back to work. Lydia decided she was too drunk to work out how she felt about that.

In the café, there was an incredible warm and spicy smell. Lydia pushed through into the kitchen and found Angel presiding over a gigantic pot of soup.

'How do you feel about getting CCTV here? Also,' she stepped closer to the delicious aroma. 'What is that?'

Angel didn't answer, but she plucked a bowl from a shelf and added a ladleful before handing it to Lydia. 'No cameras,' she said. 'Charlie said no point.'

'I'm not Charlie,' Lydia replied, ignoring the dip in her stomach. She wasn't Charlie Crow, right enough. Or Henry. Or even third-cousin-twice-removed Phoebe. She was Lydia Crow, damp squib extraordinaire and she had would-be killers and Foxes strolling into her home, casually adding doors she didn't need or want. 'We could use some dummy ones down here, at least,' Lydia said. 'Better than nothing.'

Angel shrugged.

'Did Charlie give you a budget for the renovations?'

Angel looked guarded. 'Yeah. He's booked everything, though. I'm just on site to make sure everything carries on without a problem.'

'And to make incredible food,' Lydia had been unable to resist the scent any longer and had dipped a spoon into the bowl. The layers of flavour from the tomatoes, garlic, onion and chilli, with the earthy notes of lentils and a bright green basil, combined in a smooth, creamy base that wasn't too acidic nor too cloying. It was like every childhood bowl of comforting tomato soup Lydia had ever eaten, but a thousand times better. 'Seriously,' Lydia waved the spoon. 'This is the best thing I've ever eaten. Ever.'

Angel didn't smile but there was a slight softening around her eyes. 'It's just soup.'

'I'm going to need some cash,' Lydia said. 'For some additions to the flat.'

Angel turned away and selected an onion from a basket. 'You'll have to ask your uncle.'

Lydia pushed through the door to the cafe. She opened the till and took out four fifties.

Angel was right behind her, onion still in hand. 'I'll have to tell him,' she said.

'Not a problem,' Lydia said. Uncle Charlie had told her that he wanted her to feel safe. Lydia knew exactly what that required. 'I'll keep my receipts.'

THE NEXT MORNING, Lydia woke up and swigged water. She felt fine, which was the upside to daytime drinking. The fifty-pound notes from the cafe till were on her bedside table, next to a half-full pint glass of water.

She showered and got dressed, ignoring the fact that she hadn't replied to Karen, yet. When her phone rang, showing Karen's number, she turned it face down. Carefully not thinking too much about what she was doing, Lydia went downstairs to the abandoned office. The desk and chair were both basic IKEA models, but the chair was padded and better than sitting on her bed. She unscrewed the legs from the desk to make it easier to manoeuvre and then lugged both pieces of furniture up the stairs and into her flat. She reassembled the desk in the middle of the room and put the chair behind it, facing the door and with her back to the window. It wasn't pretty, but it was functional. And since she had a proper job to go back to and this was just temporary, functional was all she needed. A very small part of Lydia knew that she wasn't being entirely honest with herself, but she drowned it with a large mug of coffee and went shopping.

Three hours later, Lydia was admiring her handiwork. Empty camera cases, just for show, in the cafe and the corridor leading to the customer toilets. Top-of-the-range wireless cameras on the stairs and outside her front door and by the back entrance to the cafe, by the bins, with a live feed to her laptop. Charlie might render the footage useless if he came near, but hopefully he wouldn't short them out unless he actually touched them.

SITTING IN HER MAKESHIFT OFFICE, Lydia checked her email and found a response from Verity. She confirmed that she met with Maddie on the fifteenth and left a contact phone number. Lydia dialled straight away.

'Yes?'

'This is Lydia Crow, I'm calling about Madeleine.'

There was a lot of traffic noise and Verity's voice was hard to make out. 'Sure.' She sounded breathy, too, like she was speed-walking while speaking.

'You said you haven't seen Madeleine since the fifteenth. Have you heard from her at all?'

'No,' Verity said. 'I told your uncle the same thing. I met Maddie for a coffee on the Tuesday afternoon. She wasn't at all contrite and I was a bit cross with her. I didn't stay long and it wasn't a particularly warm parting.'

'You argued?'

'A bit, I suppose.' Verity's voice suddenly came through more clearly as she entered a quieter environment. 'Honestly, I reached out because I thought Ivan must have tried something on, he's an absolute sod for that, and I wanted to check she was okay. Maddie laughed at me.'

'She laughed?'

'Not very nicely,' Verity said.

'How would you characterise her mood?'

There was a short silence. 'Giddy. Like she had just won the lottery or something.'

Lydia thanked Verity then headed to Charlie's house. She could call him, she knew, but she wanted to look him in the eye while she asked him a few questions.

CHARLIE LIVED on Grove Lane in a Grade II listed Georgian three-storey terrace which was set back from the street with an impressively long front garden. It was well-stocked with trees and bushes, adding an air of privacy and mystery. The foliage was alive with birdsong as Lydia walked up the path. The harsh warning call of a corvid sounded above the others and Lydia saw three magpies in the copper beech to her left. 'Good morning,' she said, minding her manners. Another four magpies flew down and lined up along the path, eerily quiet. Watching.

Lydia lifted a hand to press the doorbell but the door opened before she made contact. Charlie was standing in jeans and a white T-shirt, a piece of toast in one hand. 'Good to see you, Lyds,' he said through a mouthful of crumbs.

'I'm not stopping,' Lydia said, walking through the hallway with its original arched architrave and glass fanlight and into the living room. Bare white walls, stripped oak floorboards with a hand-knotted rug and three enormous wooden-framed windows filling one wall. A couple of comfortable chairs and a teetering pile of books were the only pieces of furniture, indicating that Charlie didn't do a lot of entertaining in this room.

He didn't take a chair, crossing to the empty fireplace instead and leaning against the wall next to it. 'To what do I owe the pleasure?'

'You didn't tell me that you spoke to Verity. How did you find her?'

'I knew Maddie worked at Minty PR and the boss there was very helpful in providing names of everyone she had been friendly with.'

'Any reason you didn't tell me?'

Charlie smiled. 'Just a little test,' he said. 'I was curious as to how you would get on on your own.' He finished the last bite of his toast and dusted his hands on his jeans.

Lydia tamped down on her irritation. 'So you knew that she had lost her job at the PR place. Do you know where she was going every day? She was leaving the house like normal, her parents none the wiser.'

Charlie shrugged. 'I don't know.'

There was the tiniest flicker of his eyes as spoke. Barely noticeable, just a tightening of the muscles, but Lydia felt a cold certainty settle in her stomach. He was lying.

Lydia waited, leaving a space for him to keep talking. Nothing. Finally, she said; 'I thought you wanted Maddie found?'

'Come on, Lyds. Of course I do.'

'Then don't play games.' Lydia narrowed her eyes at him.

Charlie smiled back, friendly as a shark. 'Got any news for me?'

'The man who attacked me was Russian,' she watched his face for a flicker but didn't find one. 'Which you probably found out before you killed him.'

Still nothing. Charlie was good.

'Which is interesting given that Maddie had an altercation with a Russian businessman called Ivan Gorin. I would say that one of the Russian gangs was targeting Crows if it weren't for the fact that he should have been in the hospital and Maddie walked away without a scratch. At least as far as we know... Daisy and John certainly didn't mention any injuries or trauma.'

'People should know better than to come at a Crow,' Charlie said, with some satisfaction. 'Anyone else on your radar? Any leads?'

Lydia decided not to tell him about Paul Fox. Not while her gut was screaming at her that she was missing something big, something she didn't understand, yet. 'Why aren't you more worried about Maddie? What else do you know?'

'Nothing, I swear.'

'Your word means less and less,' Lydia said and left before she could do any more damage. Fighting with the most powerful member of the Crow Family wasn't a good idea even if he was her uncle.

LYDIA'S FACE WAS FREEZING. She woke up with the sensation of ice on her cheeks and nose and, as she become fully conscious, her brain registered that the air she was inhaling was that of a midwinter day. In Scotland. On a mountain. Buried childhood instincts deep in her subconscious had worked out the problem before she opened her eyes, so she managed to make only the smallest of expressions of surprise. Jason was leaning over her, his face crumpled with concern. 'You were talking,' he said.

'Good morning,' Lydia said, pleased with her calmness. 'Would you mind, perhaps, not leaning over me while I sleep? In fact, maybe you could respect my privacy and not hang about in my bedroom at all?'

'What if you invite me?'

'That would be different.' And was never going to happen.

'So,' Jason said after a pause. 'Do you want to know what you were saying?'

Lydia sat up, clutching the duvet to her chest. 'What?'

'About Fleet.' Jason moved to the end of the bed and sat down. 'I think you might have some unresolved feelings.'

'Shut up.' Lydia closed her eyes. 'Eavesdropping is bad enough, but you're supposed to be sneaky about it. You can't *tell me*.'

'I'm an honest guy,' Jason said, shrugging. The movement was odd.

Lydia rubbed a hand over her face, trying to wake up properly so that she could deal with the ghost. 'Seriously. You need to stop appearing like this. It's not good for my health.'

'Sorry.' Jason looked genuinely contrite. 'I heard you shouting and thought someone might have broken in again.'

'Oh.' Maybe it was a sad indictment of Lydia's life, but she was touched by the ghost's concern for her welfare.

'I wish I could help,' Jason was saying. 'I wish I could do something. Hitting that guy, it was a rush. It was scary but then I actually did something. I affected things, you know? Changed the world in a small way.'

Oddly, Lydia did know. First case she worked with Karen, when she got a result it was like she had finally found something which made a difference. It wasn't glamorous but gathering the evidence on a cheating husband so that the wife could begin to move on was something.

Jason had his head tilted and was staring at her.

'What?' Lydia wiped her face with one hand, wondering if she had visible sleep-drool.

'There is something different about you.'

'I don't think so.'

'No, there definitely is.'

'Jason. Seriously, I don't mean to be rude, but I just woke up.'

'Got it,' Jason said. There was a pause and he looked confused.

'What is it?' Lydia stretched, feeling her spine cracking.

'When I want to move around, I just move. It's like tele-porting in Star Trek and it's about the only cool thing in this whole gig.'

Lydia waved a hand. 'So teleport. I release you.'

He pulled a face. 'Very funny. I can't.'

'Maybe if you try again?' Lydia said. She wanted to get up, shower, and drink a litre of coffee.

'Let me see,' Jason stood up and went to the wall. He put both hands against the surface and pushed. 'See?' He looked around. 'I'm not going through it.'

'I'm sorry?' Lydia tried.

'No, no, not sorry. I couldn't touch anything before you came. I could move around this place just by blinking and I could walk through the walls like they were smoke. But I couldn't touch things. I couldn't pick anything up. Not even a pencil.'

'Okay.'

'And when you got here I picked up that pot. I wrestled with that man. I had to concentrate really hard and I felt my hands kind of wanting to slip through him, but I managed to do it. I lifted that plant pot and I pushed that man and I could feel them.'

'And I'm very grateful,' Lydia began. Jason's pale face had two high spots of red on his cheeks and a hectic look in in his eyes. He began to pace, throwing his arms around as he spoke.

'I thought it was the adrenalin or something, which is stupid because I don't have adrenalin anymore. I don't have a body, but I thought it was the situation, but it wasn't. It's you.' He looked at Lydia. 'When I'm near you, I don't even have to try to remember that things should be solid, I don't have to try. Look.' He slapped the wall with the flat of his hand.

'It's not me,' Lydia said. 'I'm not doing anything. I promise.'

Jason smiled at her. 'It's okay. I like it. I'm going to get you some coffee.'

'Oh, thank God,' Lydia said, forcing a smile.

The ghost opened the door and with a final, manic grin, swept from the room.

LYDIA'S PHONE buzzed with a text message. It was Fleet asking to meet her at the park for 'a quick chat'. Lydia tapped out 'bridge to nowhere 30 mins' and hit 'send' before she could talk herself out of it.

Fleet was waiting by the ironwork steps and he was either off-duty or trying to give that impression. 'Sports-wear?' Lydia said as she reached him. 'Dress-down Friday?'

'I'm not at work.'

'You're a copper,' Lydia said. 'You're always working.'

'Fair enough,' Fleet said, smiling. 'Same goes for you, right?'

Lydia didn't answer for a moment. It was taking every bit of concentration Lydia could muster not to reach out and touch him. The sport clothes weren't for show and he had obviously been working up a sweat. It ought to have been disgusting but Lydia wanted to go up on tip-toe and bury her nose in his neck, to lick his beautiful skin and, quite possibly, do something that would get them both arrested for public indecency. As a result, her tone was sharper than she intended. 'I'm not supposed to talk to you.'

'Then don't,' Fleet said, warm eyes never leaving her face.

'You're not supposed to say that,' Lydia said, looking away.

'Because I'm a copper?'

Lydia nodded. 'You tell me I have to talk to you and then I have no choice.' The words were out and she wanted to snatch them back. Family first.

'I want you to stay safe.'

'Won't you offer police protection?'

It was Fleet's turn to nod, his face serious.

She gave him a thin smile in return. 'And we both know how effective that would be.'

'Depends on the threat,' Fleet said. 'There are limits.'

Lydia blew out a rush of air, trying to release the tension in her body. 'I wish we could talk properly.'

'Have a time out? I know.'

In unspoken agreement, they took the steps and walked to the middle of the bridge. Fleet leaned against the side and looked at Lydia like he wanted to say something.

'You mentioned pressure,' Lydia said. 'Is that coming from my family or somewhere else?'

'Hard to pinpoint the exact origin.'

'But you have your suspicions?'

'I do.' Fleet paused while a jogger went past, headphones in and oblivious to the world. 'Thing is,' he said and stopped.

'What is it? Tell me,' Lydia moved closer. 'Please.'

'About six months ago, I had a nuisance problem. A nice rich girl turned repeat offender. Drunk and disorderly, dangerous driving, property damage.'

'Women get written up for drunk and disorderly for non-violent offences more often than men.'

'Is that so?' Fleet shook his head slightly. 'Not my personal experience. Anyhow, this girl rear-ended a car. We got her for that one because she'd been using her mobile phone while driving. Logs showed it clearly, but she got let off with a caution.'

'Is that usual?'

'For a rich white girl on a first bookable offence when nobody got seriously hurt? Sure.'

'Let me guess,' Lydia said, a stone in her stomach. 'The caution didn't work?'

'Correct,' Fleet said. 'Thing was, nobody involved in any of the minor incidents wanted to press charges. In fact, they all claimed that they had been at fault, instead.'

Crap. That sounded like intimidation. In short, like the bad old days of the Crow Family, back before they decided to go legit.

'Next, she took her perfect storm into town and broke a chandelier at the Dorchester. That's the kind of acting out that gets you noticed and, along with her arrest record, it was looking good for the CPS to finally get a conviction and get her moved off my manor.'

'And you were pleased about that.'

Fleet's shrug was almost imperceptible. 'I didn't much care. It's just the job. But, yes, I marginally prefer a finished case to an ongoing one.'

'Good for your numbers.'

'Oh, yes. I'm a very modern copper. All about the stats.'

'So, what happened?'

'Top brass indicated it wasn't a desirable outcome.'

'No prosecution?'

'No.' Fleet took a swig from his water bottle. 'But what's fifteen hours of police work between friends? Drop in the ocean.'

'You're not bitter.'

He gave her a dazzling smile. 'Never.'

Lydia knew there was only one reason Fleet would be off-loading this particular nugget of work-related disappointment. 'The rich girl was a Crow,' she said, making it a statement rather than a question.

He nodded, the smile gone as quickly as it had appeared.

'And you think my uncle has some influence with your superiors?'

Fleet shrugged. 'It's one explanation.'

'Can you give me her name?'

'Madeleine Crow.'

CHAPTER FIFTEEN

Aunt Daisy was crossing the car park attached to her gym, keys in one hand and a sleek pale blue bag over her shoulder. She was wearing yoga pants and immaculate trainers and her hair was perfectly dry and styled. Lydia stepped out of her car and called to Daisy.

She turned and stopped, reluctance evident in her posture. 'I'm late,' Daisy said. 'Can this wait?'

'Not really,' Lydia said, taken aback by Daisy's casual attitude. Where was the crying woman she had met three days ago?

Daisy looked at her watch. 'What is it?'

'You weren't entirely honest with me about Madeleine.'

'I beg your pardon?'

'Look,' Lydia glanced at a muscle-bound man in too-little Lycra who was heading toward the gym. 'Do you want to talk in my car?'

Daisy looked around. 'Fine.'

Lydia shoved the fast food wrappers off the front seat and enjoyed the sight of Daisy attempting to control her expression of disgust as she looked around at the car's interior. Along with the empty crisp packets, some of which contained mouldering apple cores, there were three half-finished bottles of water, juice and high-energy caffeinated 'buzz' lemonade, a fleece blanket and pillow, and a roll of kitchen towels. She had spent long hours in this car on surveillance duty and it showed.

'How many times was she arrested?'

The corners of Daisy's mouth turned down. 'That didn't happen.'

'What didn't happen?'

'She was a bit silly. Got in with a bad crowd.'

'Who?'

Daisy looked away. 'I don't know their names.'

'She rear-ended a car. Everyone walked away, luckily, but she was done for using a mobile while driving.'

'Maddie wouldn't do that. She knows better. She got full marks on her theory exam.'

'Her mobile phone log showed a text message was sent in the minute before the crash.' Lydia flipped open her note-book. 'Now, I need you to explain to me what happened? Why didn't she even get points on her licence? She crashed into another vehicle and the other driver suffered whiplash. She was lucky not to get it upgraded to dangerous driving and end up at Crown Court. Along with her other offences, she was lucky not to end up in prison.'

Daisy's lips were compressed into a line and she wouldn't look at Lydia.

'I can't help if you don't give me all the facts. I'm not judging Madeleine, we all make mistakes.'

'Oh, I know that,' Daisy said. 'Nobody judges Madeleine. Everyone blames me.'

'I'm not in the blame business,' Lydia said. 'I'm in the finding Maddie business. That's all.'

Daisy looked at her then. Lydia thought she saw a soft-ening of her expression but the words which followed were dripping with venom. 'You're being used by Charlie to remind me that I owe him. To keep an eye on me. Well, you can run back and tell him that I got his little message.'

'I'm not –' Lydia stopped. 'Wait. What? Was it Charlie who settled things after Madeleine crashed her car?'

'Stop playing dumb,' Daisy pulled her gym bag close to her body, hugging it like a security blanket. 'Who else has that kind of sway?'

'Tristan Fox.'

Daisy's mouth actually fell open. 'Have you gone completely mad?'

'Maddie was seeing Paul Fox. It's possible his father stepped in and fixed things for her.'

'No. No. No.' Daisy shook her head so violently, Lydia worried she was going to bash it against the window. 'She wasn't. She would never.'

'I did,' Lydia said. 'When I was the same age as Madeleine. He's very persuasive.'

Daisy sniffed, opening the car door. Before getting out, she delivered a final thought on the matter, her voice rich with scorn: 'That was you. My Madeleine has more sense.'

LYDIA KICKED the front door closed and threw herself into the swivel chair behind her desk. She produced her gold coin and flipped it into the air, over and over again, until she felt calmer and Daisy's voice, her tone of disgust, was no longer reverberating around her skull.

Lydia checked Maddie's social media for activity without much hope and wondered what else she could do. She didn't know why Daisy's poor opinion of her hurt so badly, but being stuck in her investigation certainly wasn't helping matters. Frustration bubbled inside and the half-empty bottle of bourbon on the kitchen counter was calling, so when she heard footfall on the landing and saw a shadow loom through the frosted glass of her front door, she was ready for a fight. 'Go away,' she shouted before the visitor could knock.

The door opened and Fleet stood in the entrance, looking around the room with that searching gaze she found so bloody annoying.

'I'm not in the mood for an interrogation,' Lydia said, giving him her full 'off you fuck' stare. 'And how did you get up here, anyway?'

'Angel let me in. Said you were taking on clients and that I might have to wait in a queue,' he looked around pointedly at the empty room. 'Looks like she exaggerated.'

'Hell hawk!' Lydia stood up. 'Excuse me, Fleet, I need to go and shout at a cook.'

'Why do you do that?'

Lydia stopped moving. She was halfway out from behind the desk and she suddenly realised that it would be better to have the thing in between them. 'Do what?'

'Call me Fleet.'

'I told you before, Ignatius is a ridiculous name. Besides, it evens things up.'

'How so?'

'You always think of me as 'Crow' before you think 'Lydia.'

'That's not true,' Fleet said, taking a step closer.

Lydia had thought that the room was big and empty. Practically draughty, in fact. Suddenly it felt very small.

'I think 'Lydia',' Fleet said. Then he smiled. 'Closely followed by 'pain in the arse'. Is that better?'

'Charming,' Lydia said, forcing herself not to move. She didn't want him to see the effect he had. There was something about him and she was seriously beginning to wonder if the small gleam she caught off his skin was something stronger. Maybe he had Bacchus in his heritage, not just one of the families. She frowned, caught by the thought. 'What's your mother's maiden name?'

'Kamara.' He took another step and held a hand out. 'Are you going to come around to my side?'

'What?'

He tapped the top of the desk. 'There's something between us and I don't like it.'

'You're being weird,' Lydia said. Her heart was racing and every nerve ending was tingling, but it was no longer frustration and anger she was feeling. Without intending to do so she put her hand into his and felt his fingers close. Her hand practically disappeared and she stared at his beautiful hand and wrist for a moment before dragging her gaze back to his face. 'I don't know what has got into you, but –'

'Me neither,' Fleet shook his head gently. 'This is not the way I do things. Normally.'

'You do this a lot?' They were still holding hands and Lydia almost gasped out loud when he pressed a thumb into the soft base of her palm.

'Never,' Fleet said. 'I don't even know what I'm doing now. Just following my gut for once.'

'That's not always a good idea,' Lydia said.

He let go of her hand instantly. 'You want me to leave?'

'I don't know what I want,' Lydia lied.

He was smiling at her in a way which suggested he knew exactly what he wanted and that, if she gave him the chance, he would be able to persuade her to want it, too. Who was she kidding? She already wanted it. Wanted him.

'Come here,' he jerked his head a little, his voice very low and very soft. Lydia thought it was probably the single most erotic moment of her life. Certainly the most erotic of the last couple of years.

'I've decided to follow my instincts where you are concerned.'

She walked around the desk, keeping one hand on the surface to steady herself. 'Is that a fact?'

As soon as she crossed to his side, Fleet wrapped his

hands around her waist and lifted her onto the desk, so that she was sitting on the edge and he was standing between her jeans-clad legs.

'No way,' Lydia said, trying to keep her cool, going for a world-weary 'not again' vibe. 'Cliche much?'

Fleet smiled and kissed her until stars exploded in her brain. She came back to herself moments later with the realisation that she was pressing against him hungrily and holding the back of his head to keep him in place. 'Fuck.' She said, flushed with lust and embarrassment at her reaction and then a bit more lust on top.

'Is that all you've got, cliche girl? I was hoping for some Keats.'

'Shut up, Fleet,' Lydia said and pulled him back for round two.

CHAPTER SIXTEEN

Lydia sent Fleet home and slept the deep and satisfied sleep of a woman who had recently had head-banging sex. When she woke up to the sound of voices, doors slamming and a radio blaring downstairs the glow was so strong that there was a split second before she was furious.

Lydia pulled on her jeans and a stretchy black vest top, tied her messy hair into a high pony tail and marched down to the café. There were at least eight people, only one of whom she recognised. 'Angel. What the fuck?'

Angel's arms were full of catering-size tubs. 'Bit busy,' she said.

A man with a tool belt and a spanner in one hand stepped up. 'I've sorted the leak in the gents, replaced the dodgy urinal, and adjusted the ball cocks.'

'Come through,' Angel indicated the kitchen. 'The new sink has arrived.'

Lydia switched off the radio which was blaring. 'Stop. Everybody stop right now.'

'What?' Angel put hands on her hips. 'You've got a problem, take it up with your uncle.'

'He said no renovations. He said low key. He said I just

had to flip the sign a bit, make this place look legit.' Lydia waved her arms around. '*Look* legit. Not actually be a working cafe.'

Angel shook her head. 'Well, then. You're stupider than you look.' She turned back to the plumber. 'Sink, in there. I haven't got all day.'

'I live here,' Lydia said. 'This isn't right.'

Angel was already halfway through the door to the kitchen but she paused long enough to give Lydia an appraising look. 'Is that a fact?'

'I am not running a cafe.'

'You're not,' Angel said. 'I am. You don't like living above one, take it up with your landlord.'

UPSTAIRS, Lydia laid back down on her bed and stared at the ceiling, trying to work out whether to go back to sleep or go out for breakfast. Toast sounded good but the urge to pull the duvet over her head and block out the day was almost overwhelming. Her mobile began playing The White Stripes. Unknown number. 'Yes?'

'Hear me out.'

'Paul.' Lydia closed her eyes.

'I've got a job for you.'

'And I've got something for you,' Lydia said, thinking of another knee to the goolies.

'Sounds interesting.' Paul Fox's voice was suddenly warm and she could hear him smiling. An image of Paul smiling at her across the table in the Italian restaurant he had taken her to when they were dating appeared in her mind. The colours were bright and, at once, she could smell the garlic and hear the gentle clatter of cutlery on china. A warm fuzzy feeling enveloped Lydia like a fleece onesie. Hells bells, Paul Fox was good. Lydia reached out and plucked a gold coin from thin air and pressed her finger pads into the

180

cold ridged surface of the disc. Instantly the restaurant sounds disappeared and Lydia felt the feeling of calm comfort drain away.

'Is it a present?'

Paul's voice was teasing, sexy, and Lydia could practically see the charm coming out of the speaker of the phone. She gripped the coin in her palm and said: 'It's the middle finger of my right hand.'

A pause. Then Paul rallied. 'I need your help. Not a favour, I can pay. I'm sending round a file.'

'I'm not for hire. Don't send anything.'

'That's not a good business attitude. Most firms fold within the first three years, as a start-up you need all the client money you can get.'

'I've got a job,' Lydia said. 'I'm not starting my own firm.'

'That's not what your new door says.'

Lydia wondered if it was too early to start drinking.

DECIDING that it was time she started to make healthier choices, Lydia called Emma instead. She answered, breathless. 'School run, can I call you back?'

'I didn't know that was a literal term,' Lydia said. 'Can't you walk it instead?'

'So funny,' Emma said. 'You okay?'

'Yeah, fine. All good. I'll call you later.'

LYDIA LOOKED AT HER PHONE. She had wanted to complain about Paul Fox and his arrogance, the way he couldn't wait to phone her and gloat about the door, the way he was still needling her, now. He wouldn't answer her questions about Madeleine, probably had something to do with her disappearance, but was so sure of his protected position in the

Fox Family, so sure that she couldn't touch him. Lydia stopped. He had phoned her. Twice. From his mobile.

Paul Fox had called her twice and she, Lydia Crow, was an idiot.

She dialled before she could change her mind. 'I need a favour.'

CHAPTER SEVENTEEN

'I'm working,' Fleet said.

'That's handy,' Lydia was walking fast, dodging pedestrians. 'I'm coming to see you.'

'That sounds serious. I'll meet you outside.'

Lydia looked at her watch. It was almost twelve. 'If you meet me in The Hare I'll buy you a drink.'

There was a pause and Lydia stopped walking, mentally crossing her fingers.

'Interesting,' Fleet said, his voice giving nothing away. 'See you in fifteen.'

Forty-five minutes later, Lydia had drained half of her bottle of lager and had told two men that she wasn't interested in joining them for lunch. Or a drink. Or anything at all in this lifetime.

The door opened, finally revealing Fleet. 'You're late,' Lydia said.

'Didn't you call me and ask for a favour?'

'So?' Lydia stood up. 'No excuse for tardiness.'

'Tardiness?' His lips quirked into a smile.

'Do you want a drink or not?'

'I'm fine,' Fleet said, sitting down. 'I've got to get back in ten minutes.'

'Investigation?'

Fleet pulled a face 'Budget meeting.'

'Oh, the glamour.' Lydia sat down and offered her beer to
Fleet. He took a swig and passed it back.

'I have a mobile number and I need a peek at the phone
records.'

'That's the favour?'

Lydia nodded. 'I wouldn't ask if it wasn't important.'

'I'm guessing this has something to do with the thing you
can't tell me about because of your stupid family code.'

'Maybe.'

Fleet sighed and reached for her hand. 'Lydia.'

'I know it's a lot to ask. I'm asking you to trust me.'

'Everything is logged these days. I can't just put in an
action into the database and not attach it to an investigation,
not explain why.'

'You're a DCI.'

He smiled, looking tired. 'Barely. And I can't fuck it up.
My mother will kill me.'

'Family pressure,' Lydia forced a smile. 'I understand
that.' She looked at the man opposite her and felt his hand
enclosing hers. Then she closed her eyes and let her extra
sense do its thing. There was that slight gleam. It didn't
come with a warning, though. Nothing told her to stay
away, to beware. And the man had done nothing but look
out for her. He was a copper, yes, and she had only known
him a short time, but she trusted him. And Charlie had lied
to her, tested her, withheld information. Plus, he was
Charlie Crow. Hell hawk. Lydia leaned forward, lowering
her voice. 'Can I trust you?'

Fleet nodded, looking directly into her eyes.

'I want to tell you something but I don't want you to log
it or whatever. You know you said that you thought there
was some pressure from higher up when Madeleine Crow

184

got busted? That could mean one of the families has influence in the Met or even people on the inside. If it gets out that I spoke to the police about this, it would be very bad for me.' Lydia paused. 'Very, very bad.'

'I get it,' Fleet said. 'Right now, I'm not on duty and I'm not here as police. I would never do anything to hurt you.'

And Lydia believed him. She didn't know if it was the head-banging sex or her own weakness. Maybe she was kidding herself like every other stupid romantic sap, but she needed his help. She took a deep breath. 'Madeleine Crow went missing last week. My uncle asked me to find her and I've been trying.'

'Where was she last seen?'

'Coming out of her house, pretending to go to a job she had been fired from.'

Fleet nodded. 'Okay.'

He didn't ask why the family hadn't reported Maddie missing, which Lydia appreciated.

'So, I found a connection between Madeleine and Paul Fox and I have his phone number in here,' she tapped the back of her mobile.

'Solid connection?' Fleet said.

'Yes. And he is bad news but I can't tell Charlie about it because he will overreact.'

'The art of understatement,' Fleet said. 'Got it.'

'Nobody in the Family can find out that Paul Fox is involved.'

'If he is,' Fleet said, 'you are just guessing.'

'I feel it,' Lydia said. She shook her head. 'But if I'm right...'

'Badness,' Fleet said.

'If I can see his phone records for the last couple of weeks. Maybe there will be something. I don't know. At the very least he might have called Maddie and then I'll have proof.'

'Proof you will keep to yourself?' Fleet said. 'For now,' Lydia said. 'I am trying to resolve this situation without kicking off anything bigger, but I do need to find Madeleine.'

Fleet held his hand out for her phone. 'Show me.'

'You'll do it?'

Fleet looked at her levelly. 'If I was logging this as a missing person case,' he held up a hand, 'which I know I can't do, but imagine for a moment I am police and I'm following the proper procedure. Can you assure me that you have more than a feeling? That I would have reasonable grounds for accessing this man's private phone records?'

'Yes,' Lydia said. 'He was seen leaving Club Foxy with Madeleine and –'

'I don't need the details. Just your word.'

'Thank you,' Lydia said.

'Can I ask you something first?'

'Anything,' Lydia said without thinking.

'Did you sleep with me so that you could ask this favour?'

Lydia sat back. 'Are you serious?'

Fleet smiled. 'It's fine if you did. Totally worth it. But I would rather know.'

'No,' Lydia said. 'I slept with you because I wanted to and I'm asking you this because I need help and for some reason I trust you.'

'Okay, then,' Fleet said. After a moment, he added. 'Stop glaring. It was a reasonable question.'

'It was not a reasonable question.'

'Focus on the bright side,' Fleet said. 'I might piss you off but you can always trust me.'

'Get me the records and all is forgiven.' Then she leaned across the table and kissed him. Because he was there and she could.

CHAPTER EIGHTEEN

Fleet was as good as his word. The next day he handed Lydia a brown envelope with a print-out of activity from Paul Fox's mobile phone for the previous two weeks.

'That was quick,' Lydia said.

'A girl is missing,' Fleet said. 'And I have a friendly relationship with someone at the company.'

'Friendly relationship?' Lydia felt a stab of jealousy. Which was ridiculous.

Fleet smiled as if he knew. 'Just friendly.'

'None of my business,' Lydia said, which made him smile more.

'Thank you for this,' Lydia said.

'Let me know if it leads to any action,' Fleet said, his smile disappearing. 'Don't do anything on your own. If you suspect this man of kidnapping your cousin, you must not approach him without help.'

'Of course not,' Lydia said.

Fleet put a hand to her cheek. 'I'm serious. Call me. It's my job.'

'I will,' Lydia said. She was dying to look through the records, but wanted to be alone. She had crossed a line in

187

asking the police for help, even unofficially. She wasn't about to compound the betrayal by taking a unit of the Met's finest to meet Paul Fox.

Fleet clearly didn't want to go, but Lydia shooed him on his way. 'Haven't you got work to do? Crims to catch? Budgets to balance?'

With a kiss which left Lydia's mind swimming for a moment, and a final warning look, Fleet was gone. Lydia sat down at one of the tables in the window and went through the records. After a couple of minutes, when she realised the black text was dancing in front of her eyes and she wasn't taking anything in, she forced herself to slow down. Numbers and durations of calls. Without the contacts to match the numbers to, she was in the dark, and she didn't recognise any of the details. Except for her own number, of course. There were the two calls she had answered. She looked for repeated numbers and found one which had twenty-minute calls every couple of days. Family or friend or work colleague. It was a mobile number so no hint as to geographical area. She could call it, of course, find out that way. She picked up her mobile and began to enter the number. Then she stopped. There was another repeated number. On the previous three nights between six and eight in the evening, Paul had made very short calls to the same land line number. Each call was only a couple of minutes in length.

Lydia exited the phone dialler and Googled the number instead. It belonged to a Turkish takeaway in Maida Vale. The Fox Family lived in Whitechapel. If Paul Fox was calling for home delivery food, why on earth wouldn't he use somewhere closer to his house? Unless he was visiting somebody in Maida Vale. Somebody he had stashed against their will or was helping to keep hidden.

. . .

LYDIA DIDN'T KNOW north of the river very well. The Crows roosted in Camberwell, and had done since it was just a handful of farm cottages on the dirt road to Londinium, so crossing the river made Lydia feel almost like a tourist, gawping at the sights. At Warwick Avenue, she emerged from the underground station into a mild day with dampness in the air.

The takeaway was very helpful. Lydia was ready to spin her gold coin, but the guy behind the counter was bored and uncaring and he simply slid his order pad across when she asked and went back to re-doing his hair into a bun and watching YouTube on his phone. Phone numbers and addresses were scribbled alongside the numbers for the dishes. Flicking through the pad, Lydia wasn't sure how long it would take to find the number, but in the end it was easy. An address that wasn't an address leaped out. The Blomfield Road canal steps. 'You delivered here last night?'

'Not me. I don't do deliveries.'

'But someone took food to the steps? Don't you require an actual residence?'

'You pay, we deliver.'

Lydia walked to Blomfield Road. It was where Maida Vale became Little Venice, proper. Paul had ordered enough food for two people but had been cautious enough not to give out an exact address. She was tingling with excitement, even as she assessed the multiple residential properties, each one stuffed with separate flats. Door-to-door was going to take her a while. At the steps, she stopped. There was another reason, other than caution, for Paul to meet a delivery here. If the place he was staying in wasn't easy to be found. If, for example, if it was moveable.

As she took the steps down to the canal a jogger swept past on her right side and, at the bottom, a mother with a toddler waited patiently for her charge to navigate the last step.

There was a break in the cloud and the ray of sunlight made the wet pavement glisten and turned the puddles into mirrors. In seconds, they had moved again, pulling a shroud over the day and turning the shining water back to flat grey. Lydia could feel the moisture on her fringe and the tops of her ears and it seemed colder down here, next to the water. Some of the brightly-painted canal boats were covered in tarpaulins and looked shut-up for the winter while others were clearly in regular-use with plant pots crowding the roof and, in one case, a deck chair with a Thermos next to it as if the owner had just popped inside for a moment.

It was undeniably picturesque, though, even on a flat grey day. A glimpse of what the Surrey canal could have been if it hadn't been abandoned by the city planning committee, left to rot with the crumbling industrial buildings which had once stood where the park was now. Grandpa Crow was still bitter about the canal. He had shown Lydia black and white photos and waxed lyrical about tow-paths.

Lydia looked at the boats, admiring one with fresh red paintwork until something more important caught her eye. One boat, several metres away and on the opposite bank, had a plume of smoke coming from the chimney. Lydia had the vague feeling that you weren't allowed to burn fuel in central London, that it was a smokeless zone or something, but, nonetheless, grey smoke was curling in the air.

Lydia walked until she came to a bridge over the water and then doubled-back to her target. It was quieter on this side and the overhanging trees, which reached their branches towards the gentle water of the canal, could almost make you forget that you were in the centre of one of the largest cities on earth. Almost.

Outside the boat, there were no other signs of occupation. The curtains were shut tightly and made of a dark thick material so Lydia couldn't even tell whether there was

190

a light on inside. She felt a tingling across her skin. A light wave of feeling which swept over the backs of her hands, up her arms and neck until her scalp was prickling. It was like the sensation she got when there was an unquiet spirit nearby. Or when Jason tapped her on the shoulder for fun. Lydia looked around but no ghosts had appeared. The birds were still singing in the trees and a man wearing baggy board shorts and flip-flops in defiance of the weather ambled past, speaking quietly into a phone clamped to his ear.

Lydia waited for a few moments and then stepped lightly onto the small deck at the back of the narrow boat. The tingling intensified and Lydia knew, suddenly, that not only was somebody behind those closed curtains, but that they had a small gleam of power. Low wattage but definitely there. More than that, if she opened her mouth and breathed in, she could taste the power on her tongue. It was a Crow. She paused, her hand on the door to the cabin and tried to send out her senses further, imagined testing the space for others. She couldn't feel Silver or Pearl or, thankfully, Fox, but there could have been any number of non-magical humans hiding within. Although it was a small boat; how many could realistically be crouched inside, ready to take her on? Lydia shoved aside the image of scary, well-armed men piling out of the cabin like clowns from a tiny car. You are okay, she told herself. Her phone was ready, the GPS turned on and Fleet's number on speed dial. The sensible play would be to let him know where she was, maybe wait for back-up, but she wasn't sure what she was going to find and loyalty to Family came first.

The door handle turned smoothly and Lydia pulled the door open a crack. She didn't want to barge in and frighten somebody into doing something stupid. Lydia kept her voice light and friendly. 'Madeleine?'

'Who is it?' The voice was female and it wasn't frightened. It was confident with a touch of impatience.

Lydia opened the door and stepped into the body of the boat.

Madeleine, alive and well, was sitting cross-legged on a narrow, padded bench. Her silky brown hair was pulled into a messy top knot and her eyes were expertly ringed with liner, small flicks in the corners.

'Who the hell are you?'

'Lydia. I'm your cousin, but I'm here as a friend.' Lydia knew there was no point trying to disguise her identity. Even if Madeleine didn't sense that she was a Crow, there was a high chance she would recognise her from family gatherings and group photos. She opened the door wider, letting her eyes adjust to the relative gloom inside the boat.

'Shut the door behind you,' Madeleine said. The entrance led into the galley kitchen and the living space was beyond. Madeleine made no move to get up and Lydia felt she had no choice but to move through the kitchen and further into the boat. She didn't like it. One way in, one way out.

The interior was wood-panelled with red curtains pulled across the windows and multi-coloured paper lanterns strung above, giving the space a warm glow. Lydia tamped down the urge to fling open the curtains and let daylight in and edged down to the seating area. The taste of Crow was stronger in here, and Lydia could feel dry feathers at the back of her throat, and the tang of fresh blood on her tongue.

'I'm not going home,' Madeleine said. 'So don't even try.'

'Okay,' Lydia said. 'Is it all right if I tell your parents you're alive? They're really worried.'

Madeleine lifted her chin. 'No.'

'Can I ask why not?'

'You can ask,' Madeleine said, not smiling. 'Why are you looking for me?'

'Uncle Charlie asked me,' Lydia could feel that there was something seriously off about Madeleine, but she didn't know what. Honesty seemed like the best policy. 'And it's my job. I'm an investigator.'

'Not in London, you're not.'

Lydia wondered why she was so sure. 'Not usually. I work in Aberdeen.'

'You got out,' Madeleine said. 'I heard that.' She smiled for the first time and spoke quickly, getting more animated as she went on. 'Mother said you broke your dad's heart. And Charlie's. But you got out and that's what matters. I know you'll understand.'

Lydia opened her mouth to say that she hadn't let her parents think she had disappeared, been abducted or killed, but Madeleine was still talking, her hands fluttering as she gestured.

'They were always on my case, always telling me what I could and couldn't do. 'You're a Crow' and 'Family comes first'. Well, it bloody doesn't. I come first. Me.'

'What did they stop you from doing?' Lydia said, hoping to keep her talking until she could work out how best to handle the situation. The relief at finding Maddie alive was tempered by the feeling in her gut that said something was very wrong.

Madeleine shook her head. 'So many things. They had me in a cage. You don't know, you were too precious, but the rest of us, we all had to muck in.' She stopped speaking abruptly and tilted her head to one side, listening. Footsteps on the path outside and the sound of voices.

Once the unseen pedestrians had passed by, Madeleine carried on. 'Uncle Charlie said jump and everybody did. Everybody. I don't know how your dad managed to get out but nobody else is allowed to leave. So I had to run away. And they have to stay thinking I'm dead or whatever or I'll get pulled back in.'

'I'll help,' Lydia said. 'I'm not in. I'm doing this one favour and then I'm back to my own life. I'll support you, talk to Charlie for you. If you don't want to be part of the Family business, you don't have to be. The old folk all talk like it's some kind of Mafia thing, but it's not like that anymore. Times have changed. All the families have integrated and calmed down. It's not like it used to be.'

Madeleine snorted with laughter. 'Is that what your parents told you?'

Lydia decided to ignore the laughter. 'Them,' she said evenly, 'and Charlie.'

'Well they're all lying.'

Lydia hesitated.

'There's less power around,' Maddie swept one hand in a circle. 'You're right there. All the families are weak and their magic is diluted or, like, totally gone, but that hasn't calmed them the fuck down. It's made them want it more. The families are all really hungry. And you know what hunger does to people? Makes them ruthless.' Madeleine leaned forward suddenly, making Lydia stiffen. She wanted to take a step back, the energy rolling off Madeleine was palpable and the air seemed thick. Lydia tried to suck in a deep breath, but it seemed to stick halfway, as if her lungs were rebelling.

'Do you even know what the Crow Family business is? Have you got the first idea of what we are capable of?'

'It's a club for local businesses,' Lydia said. 'People pay in and Uncle Charlie makes sure there aren't any problems. Like a union. Or a round table.'

'Or a protection racket.'

Lydia shook her head. 'No. It's not like that. Not anymore.'

'How would you know? You're the precious princess. Henry Crow's heir. Too special to get her hands dirty.'

'I'm not special,' Lydia said. 'Quite the opposite.'

'Well,' Madeleine leaned back, the energy draining away as quickly as it has appeared. 'Dear old Charlie wanted me to hurt someone and I wouldn't and he said I would be in a world of trouble for crossing him, not doing as I was told, so I vamoosed. And I'm not going back.'

'Look. I'm sure there has been a misunderstanding,' Lydia said, feeling sick. 'But if there hasn't, then I will help you move away. Properly. I will help you get set up some-where new.'

Madeleine raised an eyebrow. 'How?'

'Well, I don't have any money, but your parents do and I'm good at persuading people to do things. I bet I can talk them into donating some money to help set you up in a new life. But I need to let them know you are okay. Okay?'

Madeleine stared at Lydia for a long moment and Lydia couldn't tell what she was thinking. Eventually she said. 'All right.'

'Shall we?' Lydia gestured to the door and something flickered across Madeleine's face. Fear or uncertainty or something else, Lydia couldn't tell.

'Not right now. I'm not ready. I'll go tomorrow.'

'On your own?'

'No, with you,' Madeleine said. 'I'll meet you on the corner and we'll go in together. They are going to hit the bloody roof.'

'They really aren't,' Lydia said. 'They are going to be so happy to see you.'

'Maybe.' Madeleine shrugged.

'Right, get your things together,' Lydia said, clapping her hands together.

'Tomorrow,' Madeleine said.

Lydia fixed her with her best sceptical look. 'Like I'm going to just leave you here on your own to do another disappearing act. You're coming with me.'

'I told you I'm not ready to face them.'

'Fine. You can stay with me tonight. Pack a bag.' If she could just get Maddie off this boat, that would be a good first step. She could work on her later, maybe convince her to speak to her parents on the phone at least.

'You don't trust me,' Madeleine said.

'I don't know you,' Lydia said. 'It's nothing personal.'

As Madeleine made a big deal out of putting some clothes into a large striped tote bag and a wide array of makeup into a silver-coloured case, Lydia stood by the door and watched carefully. There was still something off that she couldn't quite place and she wouldn't put it past Madeleine to make a run for it. 'Who owns this place, anyway? Did you break in?'

Madeleine was placing different sized makeup brushes into slots on a material roll with all the care and attention of a scientist and she didn't look up. 'It's Paul's.'

'Paul Fox.' Lydia said flatly.

Then she looked up. 'You know him?'

'Yes,' Lydia said, not elaborating. 'You expecting him?'

Madeleine shrugged and went back to her brushes. Lydia wanted to shake her and she had a sudden moment of empathy with Daisy and John.

Once Madeleine was finally ready, Lydia hustled her out of the door.

CHAPTER NINETEEN

The cafe was in darkness when they arrived and Lydia didn't bother switching on the light. There was enough glow from the street lights to find the door to the flat easily and Lydia just wanted Madeleine safely on the other side of a locked door. She felt exposed and jumpy, as if someone were going to loom out of the shadows at any moment and place a hand on her shoulder. Lydia didn't know how much of Madeleine's story to believe, but she had clearly been desperate enough to run away from a very comfortable life.

Madeleine moaned about the stairs and lack of a lift, she cast a disgusted look around the bare living room and marched into Jason's room. 'I can't stay here,' she said.

'It's one night,' Lydia replied, at the end of her very short tether. 'And you're not sleeping in here.'

'Oh, thank God,' Madeleine said, her lip curling as she surveyed the plain furnishing. Jason was sat on the bed, his legs crossed and a scowl on his face. Lydia was glad that Madeleine couldn't see him, especially when he started making rude gestures.

'Come on,' Lydia said, pushing Madeleine out of the room and back into the hall. 'This way.'

Lydia's bedroom didn't meet with any more approval than Jason's, but Lydia talked over Madeleine's objections. 'You can sleep in here or on the sofa. Those are the choices, so don't whinge.'

'I'll take the bed,' Madeleine said huffily. 'But why don't you sleep in the small bedroom?'

'I prefer the sofa,' Lydia lied.

'You can use my room,' Jason said, appearing next to Lydia's right ear and making her jump. 'No, thanks,' she said without turning her head.

'What?' Madeleine said.

'Nothing,' Lydia replied.

'Weirdo,' Madeleine was stripping back the duvet and inspecting the bedding with a suspicious frown.

Lydia left Madeleine to settle in. She didn't have a spare duvet but borrowed a fleece blanket from Jason.

'You can sleep in here, I don't mind,' Jason said. 'I will stay in the living room.'

'No. I've brought her here, I should be the one inconvenienced,' Lydia said. 'But thank you.'

'But I don't really use the bed. I don't need to sleep.'

'Honestly, it's fine.' The idea of sleeping in Jason's room was indescribably creepy. Instead, she made a nest on the sofa and read until she felt sleepy. She wanted to call her mum and dad and say 'thank you' for getting out of the Family business, but at the same time she wanted to speak to Charlie, to reassure herself that he couldn't really have done the things Madeleine claimed. Either way, she had found her cousin. Alive and well. That was all that mattered.

Lydia felt her eyelids closing so she put her book on the floor and clicked off the lamp. The sofa wasn't comfortable but she had slept on worse. Her last thought, before sleep took over, was whether Fleet would still be speaking to her after all of this got straightened out.

LYDIA WOKE with a bolt of adrenalin which switched her from deep asleep to completely aware in a single, disorientating moment. Her eyes snapped open as her brain prepared rational reasons like she had heard a noise in the street below. They fled in an instant as she saw the sleek silhouette of a giant raven standing next to her in the dark. The form was deep black against the dim light, like a hole in the universe. Lydia was too frightened to scream but a startled, strangled little noise escaped.

The large curved beak moved as the creature turned and Lydia knew that if she looked into its face she would see tunnels where eyes ought to be. It made no sense, it simply couldn't be true, but the Night Raven was in her bedroom, and she had never been more afraid of anything in her life. She closed her eyes, not wanting to see the raven's face. The smell of feathers was chokingly thick, stopping Lydia's breath, and the complete darkness was more terrifying still. She opened her eyes a crack.

The beak had gone. The figure straightened and narrowed, wings becoming arms. The creature leaned down and, as a curtain of hair fell forward, the tips tickling Lydia's cheek, she realised it was Madeleine. She had been hallucinating. A night terror. A bad dream.

Lydia opened her mouth to ask what the hell Madeleine was doing watching her sleep and giving her heart failure, when she felt something heavy on her chest. It was unpleasant but not painful but when she tried to speak her breath came out in a wisp. She tried to take a breath in order to try again, but the pressure was unrelenting and she couldn't fill her lungs.

'Hey there, cuz.' Madeleine's breath was sweet and Lydia

could smell perfume and an expensive shampoo. 'Don't try to speak, it will only hurt you.'

Her hands were on Lydia's chest and Lydia opened her eyes wide and raised her eyebrows, trying to convey 'what the actual f is going on?' with her facial expression.

Madeleine's smile was a ghost in the dark. 'I don't know where you stand in all this. Maybe you really are just trying to help, to get poor little Madeleine home to her loving parents,' she paused, blowing a strand of hair out of her face. 'Friendly warning, you had better decide. It's your lookout if you don't look where you're going.'

Madeleine didn't seem to be pushing down at all, her arms and body appeared relaxed, as if she was just resting her hands on Lydia's chest. But when she tried to pull her hands away they didn't budge. It felt as if a stack of heavy books were piled there. A pile of books with a lead weights for good measure. Lydia reached for Madeleine's shoulders and shoved as hard as she could from her prone position, but Madeleine didn't so much as sway. She was an immovable statue and the pressure on Lydia's chest had become agonising. Little fireworks were going off behind Lydia's eyes and she could see a darker dark than the half-light of the room encroaching from the edges of her vision. She needed to breathe but trying just hurt more. She could feel herself panicking, her mind jumping, kicking at a locked door. She could hear Harry's words, his description of Ivan lying on the toilet floor with blue lips. Like he had been starved of oxygen, suffocated.

At once her vision went dark, the black edges closing over until there was just a tiny circle in the centre and then a bright point of light and then nothing.

Here I go, Lydia thought. I should be more upset.

The black was calm and quiet and utterly empty. For a single second it was beautiful as everything fell away: No fear, no pain, no desire.

200

And then a voice by her ear brought the screaming agony in her body back in full force. It was her name and the voice was one she knew. 'Lydia.'

Lydia wanted to say 'hi, Jason' but, of course, she couldn't. She wanted to open her eyes so that she could see, but they were already open. There were bright pin points of light, again, little exploding stars which got bigger with each wave of pain. Lydia wanted to tell Jason to go away, that it was too late and that she would like to switch off and go back to that delicious blank screen. To fall through the darkness free and alone and with nothing hurting.

And then the pressure lifted and she was able to drag a tiny breath. Her chest screamed as it moved, but the air reached her lungs and her mind began to clear. There was Jason, his arms wrapped around Madeleine, holding her so closely that it looked as if he was a part of her. He was glowing a little in the half-light of the living room and Madeleine's expression was surprise and confusion as she felt herself dragged away from Lydia by an unseen force.

Lydia rolled off the sofa and crawled toward the door, her lungs and throat on fire as she pulled in oxygen. If she could get to her phone she could get help. She felt movement behind her and twisted to the side, just as Madeleine launched herself onto the place Lydia had just occupied. Madeleine twisted and grabbed a handful of Lydia's hair, yanking her head back. Lydia knew she couldn't roll away, that Madeleine had a good grip, so instead she moved toward her attacker.

She reached her hands up and behind, searching for Madeleine's face. Her defence training had said to go for weak points like eyes. Lydia had been an attentive student but had never really imagined using the techniques. Her arms felt weak, her fingers numb from lack of oxygen, but she tried to get a grip on Madeleine. She felt skin tearing away from her scalp as Madeleine pulled her hair, her head straining backward. Lydia jabbed her elbow back sharply, driving it into Madeleine's solar plexus and she felt the tension on her scalp release. Twisting around she punched Maddie in the face and got her knee up into her stomach.

Jason was there, too, his arms wrapped around Madeleine, chilling them both with his freezing presence. At once Madeleine went limp and Lydia moved away, drawing in ragged breaths. 'Don't hit me,' Madeleine said in a little-girl voice.

Lydia zip-tied her wrists and ankles, not fooled by Maddie for a second. Then she picked up her phone to call Charlie. Maybe he wasn't a good guy, maybe there was truth in what Madeleine had told her, but he had one big advantage over her cousin; he hadn't just tried to kill her.

Before she could focus on the screen, Jason gasped 'I can't' and disappeared. Then, as if the zip tie cuffs were made of paper, Madeleine broke them apart and sprang.

MOMENTS OR MINUTES LATER, Lydia had no idea, she forced her heavy eyelids open. Her head was pounding and even the low light in the room hurt. She was lying on the sofa and Madeleine was sitting on the rickety folding chair. Madeleine brought something to her lips and her face was illuminated by an orange flame as the tip of her cigarette ignited. No lighter. No match. Lydia's brain was working in slow-start-up mode, but she had enough energy to feel new fear. Just how much power did little cousin Maddie possess?

'I don't want to hurt you,' Maddie said, her voice quiet in the dark.

Lydia was head-to-toe bruises, her scalp was on fire and her head pounded. *Bit late for that.*

'You were my inspiration when I was little. I was excited when I heard you were back in town.'

Lydia struggled to sit up. Her chest hurt as if she had

been punched by the Hulk. There was a sharp pain when she took a breath and she thought that maybe the thin teenager opposite had broken a rib or two in their fight.

'It was upsetting that you were running around for him, but I understand.' Maddie's voice suggested the opposite. Her shoulders shrugged and she sucked hard on the cigarette. 'He can be very persuasive.'

'Charlie?'

She dropped the cigarette onto the carpet, ground it out with her shoe. That was when Lydia clocked that Maddie was fully-dressed and packed. Her bag was zipped shut and near to the sofa. 'I wanted you to know that you had been right to run away. Next time you should go farther.'

'What about your parents? They've been so worried.'

There was a pause. Lydia could hardly make out Madeleine's features in the dim light, but she could feel the rush of fury. She tasted feathers thick in the back of her throat and coughed, stars of pain exploding from her ribs.

'You could come with me,' Madeleine said. 'We are the only two in this family with any power, we could start our own business.'

Lydia wanted to say 'I have no power' but that didn't seem like a good idea. Madeleine's misapprehension might be the only thing keeping her alive. 'Thank you,' she said, instead. 'But I have a strict rule about not forming partnerships with people who try to kill me in my sleep.'

Madeleine smiled. 'I wasn't trying to kill you. I was just curious.'

'If you wanted to test me, there are better ways.'

'I don't think so. Mortal fear is such an adrenalin rush.'

'Even so,' Lydia said. 'I think I'll stay here.'

Another flash of anger. Feather and claw, the scent of blood. 'Not to work for Charlie,' Lydia continued quickly. 'But to live. Work for myself. I was kept away from the Family growing up and now I want answers.'

Madeleine stood up. 'That's a shame.'

Lydia tensed for the blow.

Madeleine shook her head. 'Answers are overrated. And I'm done with the Family. I'm going to do things my own way.'

'Where will you go?' Lydia didn't expect an answer. Not an honest one, anyway.

'I haven't decided,' Madeleine zipped up her jacket and picked up her bag. She stopped, right in front of Lydia, looking down at her. 'Don't follow me.'

CHAPTER TWENTY

Lydia had absolutely no intention of following her homicidal cousin. She moved in a dream, locking and bolting the cafe door behind Madeleine and then climbing the stairs back to her flat and sitting in the dark of the living room. After a few minutes, she located her phone and tapped out a text message to Charlie. It was late and he probably wouldn't see it for several hours, but there was no longer any urgency. Madeleine had gone.

Tiredness came in a wave and she could barely gather the energy to get to the bedroom. She didn't want to sleep in this room, though. And she had one last task before she could sleep. 'Jason?' She looked around for the ghost, waiting to see if he would appear. He didn't, but the curtain moved as if in a breeze, despite the tightly-shut window. Lydia looked in that direction for a couple of moments, willing him to become visible so that she could look into his eyes. When he didn't, Lydia kept her gaze at the approximate height she would expect his head to be if he was standing there and put all the emotion and sincerity she could manage into her voice. 'Thank you, Jason. Again.'

LYDIA WOKE up in her own bed and before she opened her eyes, she knew that Charlie was in the room. And her mum and dad. The scent of Crow was comforting although it was almost drowned out by the thick fragrance of fresh flowers. She prepared herself for a moment before stirring and pretending to wake up.

'Hello, darling.' her mum was leaning down and suddenly she was enveloped in a maternal hug, smelling her mum's perfume and feeling like a six year old again. She clung for a moment, enjoying the sensation of being safe and loved. No matter whatever decisions she did or did not entirely agree with, her mum and dad loved her. That was something she had always known but, seeing the grey tinge to her mother's complexion and the lines of tension around her eyes and mouth, she knew it on another, deeper, level than before.

'Look,' her mum said, straightening up. 'Your dad's here, too.'

Her father was sitting in an armchair that Lydia didn't remember owning. He had his feet together neatly and his hands were resting on his coat folded on his lap.

'Hi Dad,' Lydia said, struggling to sit up.

'I'm not your dad, love,' her father said. He looked around. 'I'm waiting for the bus but I'll help you look for your daddy if you like?'

'He was better this morning,' her mum said quietly. 'I wouldn't have brought him otherwise.'

'It's just the stress of an unfamiliar environment,' Charlie said, patting her mum on the arm. 'He'll be fine once you get him home.'

Lydia watched her mum lean toward Charlie for a moment, gathering strength. It was funny, but she'd never really thought of their relationship; that Charlie was her mother's brother-in-law, that they had known each other as young people with their whole lives ahead of them and now, with Charlie's brother looking around his daughter's bedroom with a bemused expression.

'How are you feeling?'

Her mum was looking at her again and Lydia tried to smile. 'I'm fine.'

'Course you are,' Charlie said. 'Tough as feathers, our Lydia.'

'What time is it?' Her dad was looking at Charlie. 'Are we late?'

'Nah, mate,' Charlie said easily. 'It's all good.'

'I'd better get him home,' Lydia's mum reached for her and Lydia wrapped her arms around her for another hug. She clung tightly for a moment and then let go. Her mum stood up and put on her jacket before helping her dad into his coat.

'Bye, everyone,' her dad said, smiling politely. 'Thanks for having me.'

Once they had gone, Charlie turned to Lydia. 'Do you need anything?'

'An explanation would be nice,' Lydia said. 'Why didn't you tell me the truth about Madeleine? You knew she was strong. And unstable. You could have warned me.'

'I made a mistake,' Charlie said. Lydia was glad she was lying down as she might have fallen over. The great Charlie Crow admitting to being fallible.

'You don't have to worry about her,' he added. 'You said she's gone and I know Madeleine, she won't be back.'

'But I do,' Lydia replied. 'She could have killed me.'

'I am aware,' Charlie said. He looked grim.

'I was trying to help her.' Madeleine's words were flooding back. The things she had said about Charlie. Her parents had always said that Charlie wasn't to be trusted but she had never, not for a second, thought that he would knowingly put her in danger. He was her uncle. He was Family.

'I know,' Charlie said. 'That's my fault.'

Lydia scooted back down in the bed and acted more done-in than she felt. She needed time to process everything and to work out what version she was going to present to Charlie. He wasn't pressing her for details just yet, but that wouldn't last.

'I'm sorry,' Charlie said.

Lydia had always seen her uncle Charlie as massive, ten feet tall at least, and three times louder than any other man. He looked smaller than usual, folded in on himself and his voice was soft. 'I didn't know,' he said. 'I swear I didn't know.'

'You made sure it was covered up. When she was drunk driving or whatever that actually was.'

There was a pause. Lydia wondered if Charlie would pretend not to know what Lydia was talking about.

'She was testing herself,' Charlie said eventually. 'She had discovered that she could make things move just by wishing and she was driving the car without her hands.'

'And texting at the same time.'

He shrugged. 'I said she was powerful. I never said she was bright.'

'You sent me after her.'

'I didn't think you would find her. Not alive.'

Lydia was shocked by his matter of fact tone. She felt a thrill as she realised that he was speaking plainly, though, and honestly. Or as honestly as Charlie Crow ever spoke. It was nice to be trusted, valued. And then she caught herself - this was exactly how he reeled people in, got them to do his bidding. Family loyalty, yes, but the flattery of being on the inside. The evolutionary drive to be inside the cave, closest to the fire. 'Do John and Daisy know?'

Charlie nodded.

'They are frightened of her?' Lydia said.

'Proud at first, but yeah...' Charlie said. 'They didn't

208

know what she was capable of and couldn't control her at all.'

'Maybe that was part of the problem. Trying to control her?'

Charlie looked tired. He passed a hand over his face. 'We all handled it badly. I didn't believe... I didn't think.' He stopped. 'I didn't think she was capable of anything truly bad.'

'You didn't realise how strong she was?' Lydia guessed. 'Even though you were training her every day after she lost her job.'

Charlie pulled a face. 'She told you about that, then.'

Lydia didn't reply.

'It was intoxicating.' He plucked a coin out of the air and began playing with it, flipping it across the back of his knuckles. 'I wasn't thinking straight. The excitement of it, after all this time. You know the stories?'

'That we used to be able to turn into crows and fly away? That we could see for miles, know what a person wanted most in the world, turn tap water into beer, and talk to each other without speaking.'

Henry and Susan may have vowed to bring Lydia up away from the Family business and Camberwell and give her a childhood amongst the normals, but Henry Crow hadn't hidden his true nature. Lydia's bedtime stories had been the same as any other Crow.

'So you know.' Charlie flipped the coin and Lydia plucked it from the air before it could land.

'It's all in the past, though,' Lydia said. 'Why should it matter now? We have real businesses and we've made peace with the other families. There's no need for anything else.'

'Need? Maybe not,' Charlie said. 'But the want of it hasn't gone away. Look at me.'

Lydia looked, then. She was still holding Charlie's coin and it grew hot in her hand, the tattoos on his arms seemed to be moving, and his eyes were all black. Holes in his face which spoke of one thing only; desire. 'You miss the old days,' Lydia said. Suddenly it hit her. 'That's why you want to open this place.'

'Partly.' Charlie held his hand out and Lydia gave him his coin. 'I also wanted to give you something to do. Here. A place you could call your own so you would stay.'

'But I told you I don't want the cafe open. I don't want people around and I don't want to spend my day making lattes and toasted sandwiches.'

Charlie's smile was rueful. 'I got it wrong. I admit.'

'Damn right,' Lydia said.

'But I was right about one thing. You do need something to do. Otherwise it would just have been one of your quick visits. Duty round of the family, couple of nights with your parents, have coffee with that sweet friend of yours and then away. Just like all the other times.'

Typical Charlie, thinking he knew best for everyone. Always trying to control the direction of the flock. 'I don't want to run a cafe.'

'Got it,' Charlie said. 'I saw your door.'

'I didn't buy that,' Lydia said. 'It just appeared.'

'An anonymous gift?' Charlie frowned. 'Somebody knows you better than I do.'

Lydia kept her mouth shut about Paul Fox. Charlie was being very open and very reasonable. Reminding him that she'd had once been bonking the opposition would not be a great idea. 'I have a place to live and a job. In Scotland.'

'It's got a ring to it,' Charlie said. 'Crow Investigations. How do you feel about staying here long-term? Rent free?'

Something deep inside Lydia said 'yes'. But her sensible side asked: 'What's the catch? And why are you so keen for me to stay?'

'No catch,' Charlie said, but his eyes slid to the left.

'Family comes first, you know that. Besides, I owe you. Need to pay my debt.'

'For almost getting me killed.'

Charlie stood up, looking very tall and very scary again. The flatness was behind his eyes and Lydia wondered if she was about to see the side of him which Daisy seemed to hate so much. Instead, he simply said: 'Yes.'

AFTER CHARLIE HAD GONE, Lydia took a long hot shower and got dressed. She spent time doing her eye-liner and tidying up her office space, deliberately not looking at her front door. Crow Investigations. Her own firm. She rang Emma. 'What am I waiting for?'

'What, now?' Emma said, sounding not unreasonably confused.

'Charlie says I can stay here rent-free, which would really help if I was starting my own business. Cash flow is tricky in the first couple of years for a new enterprise.'

'You're thinking of staying?' The hope and excitement in Emma's voice made something click inside Lydia. Yes, Paul Fox was an entitled dick who was playing mind-games. Yes, Charlie Crow was undoubtedly manipulating her for his own ends. Yes, her parents had, without doubt, been right to keep her away from Camberwell, to keep her safe. But this wasn't about them. This was about what she wanted. 'Thinking about it,' Lydia said. 'Definitely thinking about it.'

'Don't think,' Emma said. 'Just do it. Stay.'

CHAPTER TWENTY-ONE

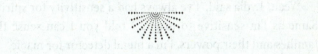

Lydia sat at her desk and opened her laptop. She drafted her resignation email to Karen, thanking her for the training and offering to help out whenever Karen needed a contact in England. Her finger hovered over the 'send' button and she was grateful for the interruption, when there was a gentle tap on the living room door. 'Yes?'

Jason came into the room, carrying a mug. He placed it on the desk and looked at her triumphantly. He looked so pleased with himself it made his face seem very open and young. And she remembered him grappling with Maddie, trying to protect her, help her. Again. A lump formed in her throat. 'Jason –'

'It's okay,' Jason said. 'We're okay. Drink your tea.'

'I like coffee,' she said, but took a sip. It was tepid and she wondered how long it had taken him to carry it from the kitchen.

'I put sugar in it,' Jason said. 'For the shock.'

'Thank you,' Lydia said.

'You look like your mum,' Jason said.

The events of the morning rushed back in. 'My dad was really bad,' Lydia said, swallowing back sudden tears.

'I think it's you,' Jason said.

Lydia felt as though he had punched her in the stomach. She sat back in her chair. 'Why would you say that?'

'I'm not being mean,' he said, holding up his hands. 'But think about it. I couldn't do anything before you came. I hadn't spoken to a single soul in thirty years.'

'Yeah,' Lydia said, 'I've always had a sensitivity for spirits. Same as I'm sensitive to magic. I told you I can sense the families and their powers. I'm a metal detector for magic.'

Jason spoke quickly. 'It's not just that. I couldn't touch anything. I definitely couldn't pick things up. I couldn't make tea.'

'So you got stronger.'

'Once you moved in.'

Lydia paused while his words sank in. 'You think I did this to you?'

'Maybe. And I think it's the same with your dad. What is making him sick? Is it Alzheimer's?'

'Sort of,' Lydia said. 'Charlie says it's to do with suppressing his magic all these years. He hasn't let it out enough and so it's turned back in on him. I mean, the Crows aren't what they used to be but I guess there's enough juice still to cause some harm.'

'If you, like, power him up, the way that you do to me, then wouldn't that make his symptoms worse when he's around you?'

LYDIA NEEDED time to think about Jason's battery theory. She needed time and space and quiet to work out whether Jason was right and, if so, how she felt about it. Instead, Charlie was determined to go ahead with opening The Fork to the public. His show of contrition evidently didn't extend to altering his plans.

Although, Lydia did manage to veto an opening party.

She told Uncle Charlie that if she saw so much as a single Time Out or Metro journalist she would be on the next train back to Aberdeen. As soon as the words had left her mouth she regretted them. Not the sentiment but the detail. Charlie would have known instantly that it was an empty threat and you should never tell a Crow something you weren't going to follow through on. Still, Charlie had nodded in a resigned fashion. 'You want to make the place fail and for your poor old uncle to lose money. I'm sure you have your reasons.'

Lydia scoured the local press and websites and scanned the local area for posters or flyers. There was nothing and when Angel flipped the sign on the front door and retreated behind the counter, Lydia opened her well-loved copy of Practical Magic and sat at a corner table, certain that the day would be a dud, the week quiet and that The Fork would have closed its doors again by the following month.

Instead, just five minutes later a couple of passing labourers popped in for takeaway coffee and bacon rolls. They looked around approvingly and one of them gave Lydia a thumbs up gesture as he left. 'See you tomorrow,' he said cheerfully.

Lydia didn't answer.

Then, as if some ancient seal had been broken, the door opened again and a woman in a suit and beige trench coat stepped over the threshold. 'Are you open?'

'Yep,' Angel said, flashing white teeth. 'Sit-in or takeaway?'

The woman looked around and said 'sit-in' before coming all the way inside and closing the door behind her. Except that there was another woman behind her in a Puffa jacket with a high ponytail. And so it continued. A steady stream of customers in the first hour so, mainly for take-away tea or coffee and Angel's pastries, but a few sitting in and filling the place with the warm sounds of cutlery on china and the rustle of newspaper.

Lydia gave up on reading and went to see if Angel needed help. 'Just this once,' she said.

'It's fine,' Angel said. 'It'll quiet down soon and I've got Leon coming in for the lunchtime rush.'

'What's that?' A woman with a sleeping baby in a sling was at the counter, pointing at a Portuguese tart and Lydia stepped behind the counter to serve her while Angel dealt with the coffee machine. It was quite fun for ten minutes or so. The simplicity of the transaction, the satisfaction of seeing someone walking away with a plate of sweet deliciousness, the glow of anticipated pleasure radiating in a halo.

As promised, the stream reduced to a trickle by ten and Angel sat down in between serving customers. Lydia saw a face in the small circle of glass in the kitchen door. Pushing it open, she felt a breath of icy air across the back of her hand so managed not to jump when she saw Jason stood on her right, peering hungrily at the glimpse of the busy cafe behind.

Lydia waited until the door had swung shut before speaking. She didn't want Angel to think she was any weirder than she already did. 'You okay?' Jason looked strained and his eyes seemed darker than usual.

'Yeah, yeah. I'm just...'

Lydia waited while Jason floated back to his position in front of the door, peering through the little round porthole. She opened her mouth to tell him to move, that someone would see him, but then she remembered that nobody else could. 'I can't believe how many people have come in already,' she said, instead.

Jason didn't look at her.

'I guess it's just the novelty value. It'll settle down when people realise it's just a bog-standard caff. They'll all move onto the next new thing.' Nothing. 'Right?' Lydia tried again.

Jason didn't move and Lydia was beginning to get creeped out. 'What's wrong?'

'It looks so different,' Jason said. 'But also the same.'

'It's clean,' Lydia said, smiling.

'Everything moves on. Everyone else gets to move on. To change. I mean, look at you.' He turned, then, and the expression on his face was desolate. 'You look happy.'

'I'm not,' Lydia said, trying to reassure him.

'You are. When you arrived you were,' he waved his hands, 'tragic. Now you have all this purpose. This intent.'

'That's not happiness.'

'I don't know,' Jason said shaking his head. 'But it's definitely different.'

'And that's not good?' Lydia was trying to keep up, but Jason was speaking fast, his voice wavering and fading in places and his outline was vibrating in the way it did when he was agitated or upset.

'Everyone changes but I'm just stuck.'

'I'm sorry,' Lydia said, feeling the insubstantiality of the words. 'You've changed, though. You're stronger than you were.'

'Amy loved The Fork. Her parents wanted to have the reception at Paco's...' he broke off. 'Is Paco's still open. The tacos there were amazing.'

'I don't know,' Lydia said.

'Well, anyway. Amy put her foot down. She said she didn't care that it was too small for dancing or that it belonged to the Crows.'

'She knew?'

'Everyone knew,' Jason said. 'But Amy didn't care. She wanted The Fork. Said it meant something to her.' He turned enormous dark eyes on Lydia. 'What did it mean to her?'

Lydia didn't answer. She didn't know.

'I've been here for more than thirty years and I've looked at every inch of this stupid place and I still don't understand. Why was this place important? And why did it have to be –' he stopped speaking abruptly, his shoulders heaving as if he was trying to take a deep breath.

Lydia couldn't move. She had never been good in the face of raw emotion, didn't know what to do or how to act. She knew her expression had a tendency to look fierce, so she concentrated on keeping her muscles soft, trying to mould them into a sympathetic expression that was genuine. Something, she realised, that was getting harder by the second as she became more and more aware of her face.

Jason stopped crying. 'What are you doing?' His voice was thin and impatient.

'I'm listening,' Lydia said. 'I'm being a sympathetic ear.'

Jason tilted his head to one side. 'Is that right? You look constipated.'

'Charming.' Lydia stopped trying to force her features into a caring expression.

Jason managed a small smile. 'I appreciate the effort.'

'Thanks,' Lydia said.

Jason wasn't vibrating anymore and he looked solid and detailed with every crease on his suit jacket and bit of stubble on his jaw clearly visible. 'I just don't know what this means. For me.'

'I could try to find out,' Lydia said. 'Not to force you to move on or anything, just for information.'

'You taking me on as a client?' Jason shook his head. 'You know I can't pay.'

'You saved my life twice. You've got some credit.'

Jason brightened a little more. 'That's true. I'm helpful. I could be your assistant.'

'I don't need an assistant,' Lydia said, which seemed more gentle than saying 'you're dead'.

'This is going to be great,' Jason said and then disappeared.

Marvellous.

Lydia didn't want to see Fleet at her office. It was altogether too close to her bedroom and she needed to be professional. She was staying in London and that meant Fleet had just been upgraded from fling to official police connection. She needed a good source in the Met and that meant no shagging him every time she felt the urge. No matter how beautiful his smile or deep and rumbling his voice or finely shaped his hands.

She watched him approach along the pavement on Tower Bridge and, thankfully, the killer smile was not in evidence. He was scowling at the world as if it had personally offended him. Unfortunately, Lydia realised with a sinking heart, this didn't make him any less attractive in her eyes. In fact, the scowl made her want him more... *Damn it*.

'This is atmospheric,' Fleet said by way of greeting. 'Why not our usual? The bridge to nowhere is a damn sight closer to home.'

'Things have changed.'

'I know,' Fleet said, leaning in as if to kiss Lydia's cheek. She didn't think she had visibly stiffened, but Fleet halted in his movement, anyway.

'Sorry,' Lydia said, feeling a bit sick. 'I shouldn't have... We shouldn't have.'

'Oh, I don't know about that,' Fleet said. He rolled his shoulders 'It's very good for tension. Stress. Circulation. Very healthy.'

Lydia smiled, grateful to him for not making it difficult. 'Well, you're going to need to get your cardiovascular exercise elsewhere from now on.'

'Is that right.' Fleet leaned back, his elbows resting on the wall of the bridge. 'And here I was, just thinking you were being dramatic.' Behind him, the Thames stretched away and the sun dipped low in the sky. Lydia felt her stomach ache with the painful joy of being home.

'So, this isn't a social appointment?' Fleet said after a moment of awkward silence.

'Not entirely,' Lydia replied. 'I wanted you to know that I've resigned from my job in Aberdeen.'

'You're staying in London?'

'For now,' Lydia said. 'And I wanted you to know that you won't be having any more trouble from Madeleine Crow.'

'Is that a fact?'

'I don't believe so, anyway,' Lydia said. 'I'm pretty sure.'

'And I should feel good about that,' he said. His tone was ambiguous, not quite a statement, but not quite a question either. Like he didn't want to ask in case he got an answer.

'It's a result.' Lydia felt him lean next to her, his arm lying next to hers on the top of the wall. She risked a glance and caught him staring at her, his eyes warm and intense. 'Not your problem anymore.'

He nodded once, not looking happy. 'You haven't asked me about Bortnik.'

Lydia looked back at the water. There was a glow spread across the bottom of the sky. She knew that in Aberdeen it would have been spectacular, the clear light of Scotland showing a hundred shades of red and orange rather than this monotone smog-choked smear, but she loved it anyway. 'Any news on Bortnik?'

Fleet didn't answer and, after a moment, Lydia risked looking at him. He was studying her. 'No new leads,' he said, finally.

Lydia made sure her expression didn't change. She didn't want to lie to him but everything was different now that she was staying. She wasn't part of the Family business, but she was part of the Family. She knew where her loyalty had to lie, where her own lines had to be drawn.

'I want you to be safe,' he said, finally.

'I am,' Lydia said. Then, before her brain could stop them, the words spilled out. 'I'm not worried about Bortnik or his associates.'

He smiled properly then, visibly relaxing. 'Good. That's good. We should go for a drink to celebrate.'

Lydia thought about sitting next to this man in the dim light of a pub, maybe in a quiet corner with a scuffed table between them and a glass of something warming and relaxing igniting the glow that she felt into something which would burn bright and hot until she was utterly consumed by it. Bad idea, her brain said. Walk away, Lydia.

'Sure,' she said. 'My round.'

CHAPTER TWENTY-TWO

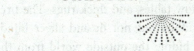

It was a few days later and Lydia had come to the reluctant realisation that she couldn't put it off any longer. An attempt had been made on the life of a Crow and if Lydia didn't manage the situation, Charlie might. And who knew where that dark road might lead?

Lydia flipped her gold coin, just once, for luck, and pressed the buzzer at the discreet entrance to Dean Street House. The intercom crackled and she gave her name. 'I'm here to see Ivan.'

'He's not here,' the female voice replied.

'That's okay, I'll wait,' Lydia said, sitting down on the step.

She scrolled through her phone, occasionally pretending to take a selfie, until the door lock clicked open.

The hall looked exactly the same as last time and Lydia wasn't surprised to see the same woman as before. Her expression suggested that she would scowl if only she still had the freedom to do so. 'You can't take photographs, here,' she said. 'Our members value their privacy.'

Lydia didn't waste time in pleasantries. She side-stepped

the brittle woman and took the stairs two at a time, ignoring the high-pitched indignation from below.

The stairs curved around and up, reaching a wide landing with several panelled doors. Only one was ajar, and Lydia trusted her instinct and pushed it open to reveal a comfortable sitting room decked out in classic club-style. Old leather armchairs, low tables, and thick rugs. The fire-place was laid with kindling but not lit and sheer blinds obscured the windows, hiding the outside world from the clientele or vice versa.

'Gorin,' Lydia said and a face appeared around the wing of one of the armchairs. It was a pudgy face, pale and unhealthy, and topped with the slicked-back unnaturally black hair that she associated with Mafia films.

'Who are you?'

Lydia took the chair opposite Ivan and sat down, causing him to raise his eyebrows. He had a newspaper folded on his lap with a pair of reading glasses on top and a half-tumbler of clear liquid on a side table. 'Vodka?' Lydia couldn't resist asking.

He gave her a look of pure hatred. 'Water.'

'Doctor's orders?'

'Again I ask. Who are you?'

'Lydia Crow,' Lydia said, leaning back in the chair. The thin woman arrived and Lydia stopped wondering what was taking her so long. She was flanked by two large men who looked as though they would like nothing more than to work off their lunch by beating something up.

'Leave us,' Ivan said, without looking away from Lydia.

The woman had her mouth open, ready to apologise or explain, but she closed it and turned on her heel, trailing goons.

'You tried to have Madeleine Crow killed,' Lydia said, cutting to the chase. 'But your man came after me by accident.'

Ivan's eyes flickered. 'I know nothing of this. I think, perhaps, you have me confused with somebody else.'

'I don't think so,' Lydia said. 'Don't worry. Charlie Crow is unaware of this unfortunate mis-step and I have no intention of telling him.'

'At the moment, I assume.' Ivan tilted his head.

'This isn't a shakedown,' Lydia said. 'It's a courtesy visit. I wanted you to know that Madeleine's actions were not sanctioned by any member of the Crow Family and that Charlie Crow greatly regrets any distress caused.'

'This is all very fascinating, but I fail to see what it has to do with me. I live a quiet life. I do not know these names.'

'I am not acting on behalf of my family in any official capacity,' Lydia said. 'But I would like your word that you aren't going to continue to seek revenge against Madeleine or any member of my family.'

Ivan seemed determined not to speak any more than absolutely necessary and Lydia couldn't help but admire his cool head. She hoped that making contact hadn't been a bad move, but she was too far along to back out, now. She had made her choice.

After an interminable pause, Ivan inclined his head. 'I sincerely regret any inconvenience which may have been experienced.'

Karen always said that a good investigator had to be willing to keep undesirables close. 'Knowledge is everything in this game and that sometimes means you have to show a friendly face to the devil himself.' Ivan wasn't quite the devil, but he wasn't far off, and Lydia fought the impulse to run from that stuffy room, down the stairs and far away. 'Good,' she said, briskly. 'And now to the second reason for my visit.' Lydia held out her shiny new business card, printed that morning. 'If you ever have need of a good investigator I'm currently looking for clients.'

225

Ivan took it and glanced down. 'Crow Investigations?' He raised an eyebrow.

'Very discreet, very reasonable, very effective.' Lydia stood up. 'I'd be grateful if you would bear us in mind.'

'You would want to work for me?' Ivan sat forward. 'I do not understand. Why would you do this?'

Lydia forced a wide smile. 'After you took out a hit on my cousin, you mean? That was personal, wasn't it? You and I, we have no personal problems. And I want to prove that to you by treating you professionally. I don't want any lingering doubt in your mind that there is any sort of vendetta or bad blood. That's the kind of thing that can escalate.' She paused. 'You know my family. I presume you know about the other Families, too. Which means you know how important a truce can be.'

Ivan swallowed and Lydia saw fear in his eyes. 'I am not looking for trouble. Not with you. Not with your uncle.'

'Good,' Lydia stood up. 'I will leave you to your morning vodka.'

She was almost at the door when Ivan spoke again. 'You said 'us'. I thought you didn't speak for your family.'

Lydia shrugged. 'I don't. That doesn't mean I'm working alone. It would be a mistake to think of me as without allies.'

'This is real, then?' He held up the card. 'You are serious?'

'Oh, yes,' Lydia said, with as much confidence as she could muster. 'Deadly.'

THE END

ACKNOWLEDGMENTS

As always, this book could not have been written without the loving support of my family and friends. Whether reading early drafts, encouraging me when I feel hopeless, or celebrating the small wins, you are all amazing and I am blessed to have you in my life.

Very special thanks to Dave, Holly, and James, Keris Stainton, Clodagh Murphy, Matthew Dashper-Hughes, and Stephanie Burgis.

Also, much love to Emma Ward for cheering me on, and letting me use her name!

A book is always a collaboration and you would not be holding this story without the vital work of my ARC readers, cover designer, and editors. In particular: Jenni Gudgeon, David Wood, Tricia Singleton, Beth Farrar, Kerry Barrett, and Stuart Bache. Thank you, all.

As ever, thanks to my wonderful agent Sallyanne Sweeney for providing expert guidance and support, and for being encouraging even when I insist on genre-hopping and doing random side-projects!

Finally, a massive thank you to you, dear reader, for giving me your time and supporting my dream.
I hope I never let you down.

ABOUT THE AUTHOR

Before writing books, Sarah Painter worked as a freelance magazine journalist, blogger and editor, combining this 'career' with amateur child-wrangling (AKA motherhood).

Sarah lives in rural Scotland with her children and husband. She drinks too much tea, loves the work of Joss Whedon, and is the proud owner of a writing shed.

Click below to sign-up to the Sarah Painter Books VIP group. It's absolutely free and you'll get book release news, giveaways and exclusive FREE stuff!

geni.us/SarahPainterBooksVIP

LOVE URBAN FANTASY?

The Lost Girls

A 'dark and twisty' standalone urban fantasy set in Edinburgh, from bestselling author Sarah Painter.

Around the world girls are being hunted...

Rose must solve the puzzle of her impossible life – before it's too late.

AVAILABLE NOW!

9 781916 465237